R. L. STINE'S

GHOSTS OF
FEAR STREET ®

STAY AWAY FROM
THE TREE HOUSE

– AND –

EYE OF THE
FORTUNETELLER

R.L. STINE'S

GHOSTS OF
FEAR STREET ®

STAY AWAY FROM
THE TREE HOUSE

— AND —

EYE OF THE
FORTUNETELLER

TWICE TERRIFYING TALES

ALADDIN
NEW YORK LONDON TORONTO SYDNEY

ALADDIN

An imprint of Simon & Schuster Children's Publishing Division
1230 Avenue of the Americas, New York, NY 10020
This Aladdin paperback edition January 2010
Stay Away from the Tree House copyright © 1996 by Parachute Press, Inc.
Stay Away from the Tree House written by Lisa Eisenberg
Eye of the Fortuneteller copyright © 1996 by Parachute Press, Inc.
Eye of the Fortuneteller written by A. G. Cascone
All rights reserved, including the right of reproduction
in whole or in part in any form.
ALADDIN is a trademark of Simon & Schuster, Inc., and related
logo is a registered trademark of Simon & Schuster, Inc.
FEAR STREET is a registered trademark of Parachute Press, Inc.
For information about special discounts for bulk purchases, please
contact Simon & Schuster Special Sales at 1-866-506-1949
or business@simonandschuster.com.
The Simon & Schuster Speakers Bureau can bring authors to your live event. For
more information or to book an event contact the Simon & Schuster Speakers
Bureau at 1-866-248-3049 or visit our website at www.simonspeakers.com.
Manufactured in the United States of America
1109 OFF
2 4 6 8 10 9 7 5 3 1
Library of Congress Control Number 2009931849
ISBN 978-1-4169-9137-3
These titles were previously published individually by Pocket Books.

STAY AWAY FROM
THE TREE HOUSE

1

For as long as I can remember, I've wanted to see a ghost. I don't think I'm asking a lot. I just want to meet one honest-to-goodness, terrifying, transparent, terrible ghost. Then I'll shut up about it.

It's really not fair that I haven't seen a ghost before this. Other kids around here have seen at least *one* spooky, hideous thing in their lives. But not me, Dylan Brown. No way. Even though I live on Fear Street, the scariest place in the world, my life has been the most boring, ordinary, totally ghost-free life in history.

But I had a feeling today was going to be different. Today was the day I was finally going to see a ghost.

Why?

Because it was definitely ghost weather today.

The morning had started out bright and sunny—a perfect spring day. But by the afternoon, heavy clouds rolled in and the sky turned dark and gloomy. Just the kind of weather ghosts like—don't you think?

Well, that's what I was thinking as I leaned back in Dad's squashy old green chair. I put the book I was reading in my lap and stared out the window. A strong wind was blowing now. And the tree branches in the front yard trembled.

Fear Street looks good and creepy today, I thought, pressing my nose against the window. *Perfect for finally meeting a creature from another world. So . . . where is it?*

It wasn't in my yard—that was obvious.

I stared left and right—into our neighbors' yards.

Nope. Nothing there.

Then I peered down the street.

And spotted something. A shadow. Darting out from behind a low bush. My heart raced—just a little.

Don't get your hopes up, I told myself. *It's probably Pokey, the neighbor's smelly old dog.*

I stared harder. It was still there. Hovering.

Maybe, just maybe, it isn't Pokey, I thought.

2

Maybe it's the ghost I've been waiting for my whole life.

Yes. This could be it. "Don't just sit here," I said out loud. "Go outside and check."

I closed my book—*The Book of Amazing All-True Ghost Stories*—and pictured myself marching across the street. I wasn't exactly sure how you were supposed to talk to a ghost. But I thought I'd say something like, "Come out now, Oh Unearthly One. Show yourself to me—Dylan S. Brown, fearless hunter of ghosts!"

A shadowy thing would ooze out from behind the bushes. As I stared at it, the thing would transform into a giant ghost-monster with glistening, knife-sharp teeth.

I wouldn't move an inch. No, I, Dylan S. Brown, ghost hunter would—

Bam!

Something behind me—something hard and icy—slammed down on my shoulder.

I leaped out of the chair, tripped over my own feet, and crashed to the floor.

"Get a grip, Dylan." My big brother stood over me, laughing his stupid head off. He held a Coke can in his hand—the cold can he had bashed into my shoulder. "You're turning into a bigger wimp every day."

I wanted to punch him in the knee. I had a great

3

shot at it from my spot on the floor. But if I did, Steve would probably tickle me.

He knows how much I hate being tickled. And he wouldn't stop until I promised to make his bed for a week.

So I didn't do anything—except sigh. Then I shoved myself up and said, "You surprised me, that's all." Boy, did that sound lame.

"Yeah, right," Steve replied. He took his baseball cap off his head and ran his fingers through his blond hair, smoothing it. Then he put the cap back on.

"I'll make you a deal. You do my paper route in the morning, and I won't tell everyone in school what a wimp you are."

I knew Steve wouldn't tell anyone. He could be a pain at home. But at school he always backed me up. "No way," I answered. "I'm not getting up at five in the morning to deliver your papers. And I'm not taking your turn doing the dishes or taking out the garbage either. So don't try to make another deal. Besides, I have better things to do."

"Oh, yeah. Like what?" Steve asked.

I pointed outside at the gloomy street. "Even you can see it's the perfect kind of day for finding a ghost."

"Oh, give me a break," Steve exclaimed. "You think *every* day is the perfect day for finding a ghost! And you haven't found one yet. When are you going to admit that they don't exist?"

"When are you going to admit that they *do?*" I asked. "There are lots of ghosts on Fear Street. Just because you haven't seen one yet doesn't mean they're not there."

I could tell Steve wanted to interrupt me. I took a deep breath and rushed on. "Remember what Zack Pepper told me? His substitute teacher was really a ghost—and she almost pulled him back into her grave! Do you think that Zack is a liar?"

Steve shook his head. "No. Not a liar," he said. "Just crazy like you."

"Well, I believe him," I said. "Every single word."

My brother laughed. "That's the trouble with you, Dylan, my lad. You believe everything you hear. When you're my age, you'll know better."

I hate it when Steve calls me "my lad." I hate it more than I hate being tickled.

And I hate it when he says, "when you're my age." Steve's only one year older than I am. *One* year. He's in the sixth grade. I'm in the fifth. And he doesn't look older than me either. In fact, some people confuse us—we look that much alike. We both have blond hair, big green eyes, and tons of freckles.

"Whatever you say, Grandpa," I shot back.

Steve smiled one of his I'm-so-much-more-mature-than-you smiles and said, "Well, at least I'm old enough to know that there's no such thing as . . ."

Steve didn't finish his sentence.

He caught sight of something out the window. And now his eyes were locked on it.

He gasped.

"What?" I cried. "What is it?"

Steve swallowed hard. I could see the muscles in his neck pop out. "A-a ghost," he whispered, pointing outside with a shaky finger.

"Where?" I yelled.

I forgot I was angry and leaped forward so fast I smashed my face into the window. My nose felt as if someone had punched me. Hard.

But I didn't care. I shoved Steve aside so I could look for the ghost.

Then I heard a horrible sound.

A truly horrible sound.

Steve. Laughing.

"It's—it's—Pokey the dog," he stuttered. "The most hideous pooch to haunt Fear Street. I guess I made a little mistake," Steve said with a mean laugh.

I flopped down into the green chair and grabbed my book. "Someday I'm going to see a real ghost," I informed Steve. "And when I do, I won't even bother telling you about it."

"I'm really hurt," Steve wailed in a high little voice. Then he gave a loud sniffle.

I opened the book and pretended to read. Maybe Steve would take the hint and leave. He didn't.

"*You* would never see a ghost even if they did exist—which they don't," he continued. "Nothing exciting ever happens to *you*. And, if by some miracle you did see a ghost, you'd probably turn around and—"

BOOOOOM!

A thundering crash split the air.

The whole house rocked.

The lamp next to my chair toppled over and the lightbulb shattered, plunging us into darkness.

"St-Steve," I croaked. "Wh-what was that?"

2

"It-it came from the backyard," Steve whispered. His voice trembled slightly.

"Let's go see."

We tore through the house and out the back door. I jumped down the steps and almost landed right on top of my dad.

"Hi, guys," Dad called. "Guess you heard the crash." He put down the chain saw he was carrying.

"Crash? What crash?" Steve said, back to sounding like his usual obnoxious self.

"We heard it, Dad. What happened?" I asked.

Dad waved his hand toward the right side of the yard. A huge tree lay stretched out on the grass. It covered almost half our lawn.

"It's time to start clearing out the trees, boys," he explained, "if we want to get our pool in before summer."

"It looks like you almost cleared out the house, Dad," Steve joked.

For once I agreed with Steve. The top branches of the tree brushed against the house. If the tree had been a little bit taller, it would have slammed through the roof.

Dad wiped a bead of sweat from his face with a rag and laughed so hard his whole body shook up and down.

"Ha-ha. That's a good one, Steve. Ha-ho-ho!"

I rolled my eyes in disgust. My father always acts like Steve is a laugh riot. He never even understands my jokes.

Dad and Steve looked at the fallen tree as if they were scientists studying a moon rock.

"I guess I must have figured out the angle wrong on that one somehow," Dad said.

Steve shook his head as if he really had an opinion about the correct angle. Sometimes my brother just makes me sick.

I wandered over to the gap in the woods left by the huge tree. I could see into a part of the Fear Street woods I'd never been in. And way in the distance I saw something amazing.

"Steve," I yelled. "Steve, you are absolutely not

going to believe what's out there." Steve didn't look up.

"Steve!" I hollered. "Come on! Look! I think I see a tree house."

"Where?" Steve actually sounded a little interested.

"There, way deep in the woods. You can just see the top of it." I pointed straight ahead into the deep woods.

"Oh, yeah, I see what you mean," Steve admitted. "It might be a tree house—but how come we never saw it before?"

"I don't know, the branches of the other trees must have hidden it. Come on, let's go look for it."

Steve yawned. "I think I'll go inside and watch some TV," he said. "Tell me if you find it."

Is my brother the laziest person in the world, or what? "No way!" I answered. "I'm going to find the tree house. And I'm claiming it for myself!"

"Okay, okay," Steve said quickly. "I'll come with you. Just to make sure you don't get lost."

I knew that would get him. Steve can't stand it if I have something he doesn't.

"Don't go too far, guys," Dad warned. "It's almost dinnertime. I'm making my rigatoni with spicy meatballs tonight. It has to be served as soon as it's ready, or else it tastes like glue."

"Sure, Dad," I answered. Then I plunged into the woods and trotted along the rocky, overgrown trail.

Steve followed behind me. Complaining. As usual. "This path is bumpy," he griped. "And it's freezing out here!"

"You're right," I admitted. "I wonder why it's so cold."

I noticed my breath making frosty little clouds in front of my face. It *is* chilly for April, I thought. And the air seems to be getting colder with every step we take.

Steve tripped over a rock and fell flat on his face. He flipped over and glared at the rip in the knee of his favorite jeans. "This path stinks!" he yelled. "I'm going back."

I grabbed his arm and hauled him to his feet. "Let's keep going for a little while longer," I begged.

I didn't understand it, but something seemed to be pulling me into the woods. I couldn't stop now.

"No! I'm out of here." Steve turned and started back to the house.

"Wait! I have a deal for you."

Steve spun around. He loves deals. "It better be good," he warned.

"I'll do your paper route tomorrow morning."

He shook his head. "Not good enough," he said. "But if you deliver my papers every morning it rains from now until the end of the year, I'll stay out here five more minutes. That's it. Take it or leave it."

"Ten more minutes," I said.

Steve nodded. "It's a deal."

We followed the overgrown path around a sharp curve—and that's when I saw it.

I stopped short and Steve bashed into me.

"What's wrong with you?" he complained.

I didn't speak. I couldn't.

I pointed to the top of a huge black oak tree standing alone in a clearing. On one side of the tree, an enormous branch rose up like a huge twisted arm, reaching up into the dark sky. Between the branch and the trunk, I could just see the remains of a platform, and a jagged section of wall.

The tree house.

"It looks like somebody dropped a bomb on it or something," Steve observed.

I trotted halfway across the clearing. "Look there," I whispered, pointing to the trunk of the black oak. "It used to have two levels. See that ladder that starts near the ground? It leads to a platform below the other one."

I noticed that half of the bottom platform was charred black. And there were no branches on that side of the tree.

I closed my eyes for a second and tried to picture

the tree house with both levels rebuilt. "This is so cool," I whispered.

"Great. Come on. Your ten minutes are up," Steve said.

I walked to the oak. Then I stopped.

I froze in horror.

Someone—or something—was standing at the base of the tree.

Almost hidden in the shadows.

It was a dark, shadowy, formless *thing* and I could see its eyes. Its cold, dark eyes.

And they were staring straight at me.

3

I opened my mouth to call my brother's name. But no sounds came out. My lips were suddenly too stiff to form words.

I silently told my legs to walk forward, toward the shapeless *thing*.

I was terrified, but I had to know whether it was a ghost. I had to find out if it even existed, or whether I was just imagining it.

But I just couldn't make myself move!

I swallowed hard three times. At last I was able to croak out a few words. "Steve," I whispered, "do you see that?"

"What?" Steve's voice rang out in the woods.

"What did you say, Dylan? Why are you whispering like that? I can't hear a word you're saying."

His words sounded so loud in the eerie silence. "Don't you see that . . . that *thing* over there by the tree?" I asked again. But before I'd even finished my sentence, the black form melted away into the shadows.

"Give it a rest, Dylan," Steve said.

"But I saw it!" I insisted, squinting at the tree. "A big, black kind of blobby shape. It was looking right at me, and . . ."

"Dy-lan! Steve! Din-ner!" My father's booming voice carried through the cold, clammy air. But he sounded so far away. "On the doub-le!"

"Come on." Steve yanked my arm.

But I was frozen to the spot. Staring at the tree. Hoping I'd see the shadowy figure one more time.

"You stay here if you want," Steve muttered. "I'm going home to eat."

"Okay, okay," I mumbled. "But can we come back?"

"Yeah, sure. We can come back," Steve said. "Another time. Like maybe in a hundred years."

Steve started back on the bumpy path. I glanced at the tree house one last time. Everything remained still.

That's when I realized how totally quiet the woods were.

No sounds at all.

Not even the chirp of a single bird.

Weird. Definitely weird.

I slowly turned and followed my brother. *I'm coming back,* I promised myself. *No matter how creepy these woods are . . . I'm coming back. This could finally be my chance to meet a ghost!*

As we hurried home, I noticed something else about the woods that was strange. The farther we got from the tree house, the warmer I felt.

Didn't one of my ghost books talk about cold spots in haunted houses? I had to read up on all the signs of ghost appearances right away!

Steve led the way inside, telling Mom and Dad, "Dylan's seeing things again." He really does treat me like a baby.

In the bright light of the kitchen I could hardly believe I'd seen the shadowy ghost out in the woods. But I knew I had. And I couldn't stop thinking about it.

During dinner I dribbled Dad's tomato sauce down my shirt. And Mom had to ask me three times to pass the bread.

I could hear Steve snickering at me, but I didn't care. The second I was excused from the table, I ran upstairs to my bedroom. I had to start my ghost research.

Steve barged into the room a few minutes later

and dropped down on the bottom bunk of our bunk beds. Then he reached into his backpack, pulled out a book, and groaned.

I already knew what was coming.

"Dylan, my lad, I have—"

"A deal for you," I finished.

"This is a really good one," Steve protested. "You write my social studies report for me, and I'll take back any rainy Mondays, Wednesdays, and Fridays for delivering my newspapers."

I noticed this deal left me with four days a week, while Steve had three.

And he stuck me with the Sunday papers.

Everyone knows those are the heaviest.

"No deal. I'll take my chances with the rain." I reached over to my bookshelf, grabbed my copy of *The A-Z Ghost Encyclopedia,* and looked up cold spots.

The encyclopedia confirmed that cold was a sign of a haunted place.

I knew it!

"What then?" Steve asked. He still hadn't bothered to open his social studies book. "What kind of deal do you want to make?"

"How about I write the paper, and you help me rebuild the tree house?" I suggested. "That—or nothing," I quickly added. I've learned a few things from Steve.

"No *way* am I helping you rebuild that tree house," Steve answered. "That would take as long as writing a hundred papers. That place is a total wreck."

"But think how cool it could be." I sat down at my desk, grabbed a big sheet of paper, and started sketching. "A two-level tree house of our own—where no one would bother us."

"It wouldn't be worth the work," Steve mumbled.

I ignored him and kept drawing. Then I held up the sketch.

"Whoa!" Steve exclaimed. "Do you really think you could make that awesome pulley thing and rebuild the second floor?"

"Sure. But I would definitely need your help on it."

That wasn't quite true. Steve would probably drive me nuts the whole time. But if the shadowy thing really *was* a ghost—and if it came back—I wanted Steve to see it. So I could prove to him—finally—that ghosts were real!

"Come on, Steve," I continued. "It'll be a cool place to hang out. And nobody could bug us about doing our homework up there." I left my chair and glanced out the window to see if I could spot the tree house.

"Hmmmm," Steve thought a minute, brushing

his hair back under his baseball cap. "Okay, I'm in."

Do I know the right thing to say to my brother, or what?

"But you have to do more of the work," Steve added. "Because you're the one who really wants the tree house."

"You are so . . ." My voice trailed off.

"So what?" Steve asked.

I didn't answer him.

I was staring out the window. Right where I thought the tree house stood.

"Look!" I shouted. "Look! There! A light—out by the tree house."

"You're probably seeing things, as usual," Steve grumbled. He rolled off the bed and shuffled over to the window. He leaned close to the glass and cupped his hands around his eyes. "Hey! There *is* a light bouncing around out there."

"Why would someone be out in the woods at night?" I wondered out loud.

"That's a good question," Steve replied.

We stared out the window in silence. Watching the light bob and flicker.

Could it be the ghost? Maybe, I decided. But why would a ghost need light?

There was only one way to find out for sure. "Let's go and check it out," I said quietly.

To my amazement, Steve didn't argue or try to make a deal. He pulled a sweatshirt out of his middle drawer and yanked it over his head.

"This time, I'm not going to freeze to death," he announced. "Come on. What are you waiting for?" Steve grinned at me and slapped me a high five.

Every once in a while having a brother can be cool.

Steve turned on the radio before we left our room. "Better have some noise in here."

Steve was right—sometimes Mom and Dad get suspicious if we are *too* quiet. Dad claims it's because they're afraid we've killed each other. Ha-ha.

I followed Steve down the stairs. We both stepped over the third step. That's the one that creaks.

As we crept through the kitchen I snagged a flashlight from the junk drawer. We cut across the backyard and entered the woods. Then I flipped the flashlight on.

It didn't help much. We both tripped over rocks and roots. We'd only gone about three feet when Steve started asking the same question over and over again.

"Why?" he chanted. "Why, why, why? Why did I agree to do this?" With each step he took, he muttered, "Why?"

I wanted to tell him to shut up. But I didn't want to make him angry. I didn't want him to turn back.

When we had made it about halfway there, Steve changed his chant. He changed it to "Cold. Cold, cold, cold."

He was really getting annoying now. But I had to admit it—it was cold. I was shivering.

But that was a good sign!

Yes. Cold was definitely a good sign.

Because cold meant ghosts!

"Do you see anything?" Steve whispered in my ear.

"No—wait. Maybe." I stared hard at the big oak tree. "There!" I pointed. "I just saw a light on that side of the tree. Then it went out."

I dug my heels into the ground—planting them there firmly—so it would be harder to bolt, which is exactly what I wanted to do.

I cleared my throat.

"Who is there?" My voice squeaked.

The light flashed again.

Then it went out.

Swoosh, swoosh, swoosh.

"D-did you hear that?" I asked Steve. He nodded.

Something was moving in the dark.

Swoosh, swoosh, swoosh.

21

There it was again. Like ghostly feet sliding over the grass. Moving. Toward us.

I swung the flashlight around wildly. Trying to catch it in my beam.

Then I heard another sound. A voice. A laugh.

"Steve, did you hear that?" I whispered. "It laughed."

"Shine your light over there," Steve whispered back.

He sounded scared. I knew I was.

I swung my flashlight in that direction—and two humanlike forms walked toward us.

Girls.

Two girls squinting in the light and giggling.

Two totally alive girls.

4

I wanted a ghost. Or a werewolf. Or a vampire. Even a mummy.

But no. I found girls.

"Who are you?" Steve asked as we walked toward them. "What are you doing out here?"

"I'm Kate Drennan," one of the girls answered in a soft voice. "And this is my sister, Betsy."

Both girls had bright blue eyes and long black hair. The one named Kate had straight hair tied back in a ponytail. The other one had wavy hair with curls that tumbled all the way down her back.

I'd never seen either of them before—even though they looked as though they should be in my grade.

"We were just—" Kate began again. But before she could finish, Betsy cut her off.

"Why do you get to ask the questions?" she demanded. "We have as much right to be here as you do."

"Okay, okay," I started to apologize. "It's just that I've never seen you around here before. Do you go to Shadyside Middle School?"

"No," Kate started to answer.

"We're on spring break," Betsy interrupted. "We go to school in Vermont. We don't know many kids in Shadyside, so it gets pretty boring."

"That's why we sneaked out tonight," Kate added. "We were bored. There was nothing on TV. Nothing to do."

"We sneaked out, too," I admitted.

Kate—the nicer one—smiled. And Betsy—the bossy one—seemed to relax a little.

"At least you get a vacation," Steve added. "We don't have one until school lets out for the summer."

"We should head back," Betsy said. "Our parents might check up on us or something."

"Us, too. We'll probably see you around," I volunteered. "We'll be out here a lot—we're going to rebuild that tree house."

I shone the flashlight up into the branches of the big, dark oak. Both girls glanced up. Then I noticed

Kate's expression. She looked scared. Really scared.

Betsy glared at me. "What did you say?" she asked.

"I said we're going to rebuild that old tree house."

"That's what I thought you said," Betsy replied. "But you can't."

"Why can't we?" Steve demanded.

"No one can," Betsy insisted.

Kate began chewing nervously on the end of her ponytail. "You can't rebuild the tree house," she said. "You can't because . . . because . . ."

"Because of the secret about it," Betsy finished for her sister.

"The secret?" I asked. "What secret?"

5

A tree house with a secret! Is this cool or what?

"We can't tell you. Everyone knows about this old tree house," Betsy snapped.

Then she narrowed her eyes. "But I *will* tell you this—if you don't want to get hurt . . . you'll stay away from the tree house!"

"They're just trying to scare us," Steve replied. "But it's not going to work. Right?"

"Right," I replied, not feeling as convinced as I sounded.

"Well, I, uh, really think you should listen to Betsy," Kate whispered. "Because we, um, we heard some kids tried to fix up the tree house and they . . ."

"What happened to them?" These girls were driving me crazy. "Did they die? What happened?"

Betsy shook her sister's shoulder, interrupting her for the millionth time. "Come on. Let's go. They don't need to hear that old story," she snapped. "If they're smart, they'll just stay away."

"Why? Why should we stay away?" I asked. Then I remembered what I had read about ghosts and cold spots. "Wow!" I said. "Is the tree house haunted?"

"Come on, Kate," Betsy ordered. "These guys are hopeless."

Kate gave a sort of half smile. "We do have to go," she said. "Our mom will freak if she can't find us."

"Wait!" I protested. "Just tell us some more about the tree house. Please!"

I thought Kate was about to say something, but Betsy didn't give her a chance. "I said come *on*," she grumbled, tugging her sister across the clearing.

"Bye," Kate called over her shoulder.

As they stepped onto the path, Betsy stopped and called back, "Remember, you have been warned. Now if anything bad happens to you, it will be your own fault!"

The next day at school, I couldn't concentrate. Betsy's warning kept echoing in my head. What did

27

it mean? What was the big secret about the tree house?

It must be haunted, I decided. That had to be it. At least I hoped so.

I spent the last part of the day—the part when we were supposed to be doing math—drawing tree house plans on the cover of my notebook.

In some of the plans, I sketched a shadowy figure sitting on the end of a branch. I made it shadowy because I didn't know what a ghost really looked like. Not yet, anyway.

As soon as the last bell rang, I raced home. I headed straight into the garage and loaded up two big cardboard boxes with nails, old boards, and lots of tools.

That was the easy part.

Next came the hard part—Steve. I found him lying on the couch, watching TV, and munching Cheese Curlies.

"Come on," I said. "We have to start before it gets too dark out there."

Steve's eyes remained glued to the screen. "Let's wait till Saturday," he answered. "I want to watch the rest of this show."

I glanced at the TV. "You've seen that cartoon at least one hundred times!" I snatched the remote from his hand and clicked off the TV. "We had a deal."

"Our deal didn't say *when* I had to help," Steve answered. "What's the big rush, anyway?"

"I think the tree house is haunted! I think someone died up there! And I did see something in the shadows."

"Dylan," Steve said, shaking his head, "the only thing that died is your brain."

"I can *prove* to you that ghosts are real," I replied. "Just think about it—this is the perfect chance for us to settle our argument about ghosts. If the tree house is haunted, I know I can prove it."

Steve shoved himself up from the sofa.

"All right, Dylan, my lad. But if we don't see a ghost before we finish the tree house, you have to admit I was right and you were wrong."

"Sure. Let's go."

"And you have to stop talking about ghosts, reading about ghosts, watching movies about ghosts—even thinking about ghosts. Deal?" Steve asked.

"Deal," I agreed.

We headed to the garage to pick up the supplies. Steve chose the lightest box, of course.

We cut across the backyard, and I led the way into the woods. "Wow!" Steve cried as he stumbled along behind me. "The woods are even colder than last night. From now on, I'm wearing my winter parka when we come out here."

"It's because of the ghost," I informed him. "Haunted places usually have a colder temperature."

"Give me a break!" Steve shouted. "It's cold because of all the trees. The sunlight can't get through the branches."

After that we trudged along without talking. My box felt heavier with every step. I thought about turning around and asking Steve to trade. But I didn't want to start another argument.

I stopped when the path reached the clearing.

I scanned the shadows around the oak tree.

Nothing there.

I dumped my cardboard box on the ground. I turned to Steve—and couldn't believe what I saw. "Where's yours?" I demanded.

"Where's my what?" Steve asked, smiling.

"Your *box.*"

Steve took off his baseball cap, smoothed his hair, and stuck the cap back on. "I left it at the edge of the backyard. We couldn't possibly use all that junk in one day," Steve explained.

"That was not our deal!" I yelled. "Our deal was that you help. Watching me carry a box does not count as help. And neither does leaving our stuff behind!"

"Okay, okay. I'll get the box," Steve muttered.

I watched Steve disappear down the path—and

realized what a big mistake I had made. I'd be lucky if Steve returned—with or without the box.

In fact, I knew exactly what Steve would do. He would decide he needed a glass of water. No, a glass of water and some more Cheese Curlies—to build up his strength. And since he couldn't eat and carry the box at the same time, he'd watch a few cartoons until he finished the Curlies. And by then, it would be time for me to go home.

Well, I didn't need Steve, anyway. I really didn't expect him to do much work. I just wanted him along because the woods were kind of creepy. Which is exactly what I started thinking as I opened the carton.

It was quiet here. Way too quiet.

And dark. Steve was right about the branches. They blocked out all the sunlight.

I glanced up at the tree house and felt a shiver race up and down my spine. *You wanted to see a ghost,* I told myself. *And now's your chance.*

I forced myself to march over to the tree. I tested the first rung of the ladder nailed onto the trunk. A little wobbly, but okay, I decided.

I stepped on the rung. It held me—no problem. I tugged on the second rung before I climbed up—it felt okay, too. Only three more rungs to go.

I stared up at the tree house again. An icy breeze swept over me and my knees began to shake.

Take a deep breath, I told myself. *Don't wimp out now.*

I stepped up to the next rung.

And that's when I heard the sound.

A sickening *crack*.

My feet flew out from under me as the third rung snapped off the trunk.

I flung my arms around the tree. I kicked my legs wildly, searching for a foothold. I tried to pull myself up to the fourth rung.

My heart pounded in my chest until my feet found it. Then I clung there for a few minutes. Hugging the tree trunk tightly, trying to catch my breath.

A cold gust of wind blew. My teeth began to chatter.

I inhaled deeply. "Okay, just one more rung to go," I said out loud. But I couldn't move. I remained frozen to the spot.

Then I pictured myself talking to Steve after I'd proven that ghosts exist. "Steve, my lad," I would say, "don't feel stupid. Even though you are a year older, no one expects you to be right about everything."

That gave me the courage to go on.

I made my way to the top rung. I peered underneath the tree house and studied the platform. Half of it was badly damaged. The boards were charred black. But the other half appeared solid enough. I banged on the boards with my fist a few times just to make sure.

Then I pulled myself through the open trapdoor—and felt something touch my face. Something soft. Something airy. Something light.

I screamed.

I found the ghost!

6

I leaped back. But the ghost wrapped itself around me. It covered my face. I couldn't breathe.

"Get away from me! Get away from me!" I screamed. My arms flailed as I tried to fight it off.

Its touch was sticky. It felt like—spiderwebs.

Spiderwebs.

I wasn't battling a ghost. I was fighting spiderwebs.

I guess that should have made me feel better, but it didn't. Because the more I fought, the more tangled up I got.

I shook my hands, but the webs wouldn't come off. And my fingers started to burn and itch.

I tried to brush the webs out of my face. I could

feel them clinging to my eyelashes. They were in my ears. My nostrils. My mouth.

"Get off! Get off!" I screamed as I clawed at my face.

They pressed in tighter.

They were suffocating me.

I couldn't breathe.

I stumbled around the tree house until I found the trapdoor. Then I lowered myself through the hole. I didn't bother feeling around for the rungs. I slid all the way down the tree trunk.

When I reached the ground, Steve was standing there. "Help me get these things off!" I yelled. "They're all over me. I almost choked to death!"

Steve pulled off his jacket and brushed the webs off with it. I grabbed it and wiped my face.

"Are you okay?" Steve asked.

I nodded.

"Then give me back my jacket."

I threw it at him. He shook it out and pulled it over his head.

Even though the webs were gone, I couldn't stop scratching.

"There weren't *that* many," Steve commented as he watched me.

"I couldn't breathe!" I protested.

"You just scared yourself," he said. "You're so

35

convinced there's a ghost up there that you freaked."

"I almost died!" What did Steve know? He wasn't the one in the tree house.

"Hey! Maybe that's what that weird girl meant when she said the tree house was dangerous," Steve said.

"What? What do you mean?"

"Killer cobwebs," he replied.

"That's funny, Steve. Real funny." I closed up the carton with our tools and shoved it up against the tree. "We'll leave it here until tomorrow—"

When you go up to the tree house first, I added to myself. *And you're the one smothered in itchy, burning spiderwebs. Then we'll see how you like it, Steve. Then we'll see.*

The next morning was Saturday. Finally! A whole day to work on the tree house. I got up early and waited for Steve on the porch. I checked my watch. Seven A.M. Steve would be here any minute.

The minute I sat down on the front steps, Steve rounded the corner on his bicycle. He rode up and dumped his bike on the lawn.

"Ready?" I asked him, jumping up.

"Yep. Ready," he replied. He plowed past me and headed for the door. "Ready to go back to bed."

"Hey!" I cried, running to the door and bracing

36

both arms against the frame to block his way. "You agreed to work all day on the tree house."

"I'm going back to sleep. I'll help you when I get up." He shoved me aside.

"Doughnuts," I said just as he turned the knob. "Double-dipped chocolate doughnuts."

"You've got doughnuts?" Steve asked.

"In my backpack. Mom drove me down to the Donut Hole."

"Hand them over," Steve ordered. "Mom didn't buy them just for you." He took a few steps toward me. Then he lunged for my backpack.

"Mom didn't buy them," I said, leaping back. *"I* did. With my own money. And I'm taking them out to the tree house."

I pushed past Steve and ran around the house. I could hear his feet pounding right behind me.

Halfway to the clearing, Steve caught up to me and yanked my backpack off. He pawed through it and grabbed a doughnut with each hand.

"You'll never be able to outrun me, Dylan, my lad," Steve declared. He took a big bite of one doughnut. Then he followed me down the path.

Do I know my brother, or what?

When we reached the clearing, I handed Steve another doughnut and took one for myself. "It's your turn to deal with the spiderwebs today," I announced.

I pulled an old house painter's mask out of my backpack and tossed it to Steve. "Wear this. At least it will keep the webs out of your nose and mouth."

"I don't need it," he said, tossing it aside. Then he began climbing up the tree.

I stared up and watched him climb. Even though it was a bright sunny morning, the tree house was cloaked in darkness. A breeze rustled the leaves. A cold breeze.

Steve entered the tree house through the trapdoor. "Oh, no!" he cried out.

"What?" I yelled. "Is it the ghost?"

"No, you idiot. I forgot to take the hammer," he replied, laughing. "Hand it up to me. The one with the big claw on the end. I'll need to pry some of these boards up. And give me some new boards, too, while you're at it."

No ghosts. No spiderwebs.

I wasn't sure what disappointed me more. I handed Steve the stuff he needed. Then I started working on a new ladder. I grabbed a saw from one of the cardboard boxes and found some small pieces of wood that I could cut into rungs.

As I sawed, I kept thinking about the spiderwebs. Maybe Steve was right. Maybe I just panicked yesterday.

But maybe, I thought, *just maybe, the ghost*

wrapped all those webs around my head. One of my books said some ghosts would do anything to keep humans away.

I yanked off the old rungs and began hammering the new ones into place. I was rummaging through the carton to find some nails when I realized I didn't hear Steve hammering anymore.

"Steve? How's it going up there?" I called.

No answer.

He better not be sleeping, I thought. *Not after I spent my allowance on his favorite doughnuts.*

"Steve?"

No reply.

"I'd better wake him up," I said, grumbling. I climbed up the first two rungs of the ladder and peered up.

And that's when I saw it.

The hammer.

With the big black claw at one end.

Plunging down.

Plunging straight for my face.

7

I let go of the tree and hurled myself to the ground.

Thwack! The hammer landed inches away from my nose.

"Steve!" I yelled. "You almost killed me with that hammer."

I shoved myself to my feet. My jeans were torn and my knee throbbed.

"Don't pretend you aren't up there," I bellowed.

Still no answer.

I scrambled up the rungs and poked my head through the trapdoor. No Steve.

"Now what are you screaming about, Dylan, my lad?" Steve stood halfway across the clearing, holding a bag of Cheese Curlies.

"How—how did you get over there?"

"I went back to the house for these," he said, holding up the orange bag. "You were so busy sawing you didn't notice." He grinned. "Want some?"

"No, I don't want some," I shouted. "Your hammer almost hit me in the head. Why did you leave it near the trapdoor?" I asked.

"I didn't," Steve replied. "I left it in the middle of the platform."

"You did not," I screamed.

"Did, too," Steve screamed back.

"Hey, is something wrong?" It was that girl Betsy. She and her sister, Kate, stepped out from behind the tree.

"We heard yelling," Kate said. "We thought someone was hurt." She tugged on the end of her ponytail.

"Someone *was* almost hurt." I glared at Steve. "Me. That thing came flying straight at me," I said, pointing to the hammer on the ground. "It could have smashed my head open."

"What thing?" Kate asked. Her eyes showed real concern—fear, even.

"Steve's hammer. He left it on the edge and it fell and nearly killed me." I was practically shouting.

"That's just what happened the last time," Betsy said.

Then they both nodded.

"What happened? What last time?" Now Steve was shouting.

"You must have made it very angry," Betsy said.

"I made the hammer angry? Are you crazy?" I was practically yelling at them. Why did they always have to talk in riddles?

"Not the hammer," Kate whispered. *"It."*

"Who is *it?*" I demanded.

"There is no *it,*" Steve cut in. "Get real, Dylan. The wind probably blew the hammer down. Or a squirrel knocked it over."

"Believe whatever you want." Betsy smirked. "But we warned you. We warned you not to work on the tree house."

I turned toward Kate. She was chewing the end of her ponytail now.

"You made it angry," Betsy said again. "It's not a good idea to make a ghost angry."

8

"**T**ell me. Tell me about the ghost," I begged.

"I guess we have to tell them." Betsy turned toward her sister. "If we don't, they'll never finish the tree house—alive."

The four of us sat down in a circle. Betsy's eyes darted around the clearing. "I don't know if it's safe to tell this—especially so close to where it happened."

"Please—" I started.

Betsy held up her hand, signaling me to shut up. Then she began the story.

"A long time ago three kids around our age built the tree house. They drew hundreds of pictures of it first—until they agreed on how it should look.

They wanted it to be the most perfect tree house ever. Then they spent weeks and weeks up there. Hammering. Sawing. Making sure everything fit just right."

"Ooooh, I'm starting to get scared already," Steve said, rolling his eyes.

"Ignore him," I told Betsy.

"The night the tree house was finished, the kids decided to sleep in it. They brought some food and their sleeping bags. And they stayed up late— telling ghost stories.

"Suddenly, a thunderstorm rolled in. Streaks of lightning cut through the sky. But the kids weren't scared. They thought it was cool to be there. A great night for ghost stories."

I nodded. I know how much I like to read my ghost books when it's cold and gray. Ghost weather.

"Then a strong wind picked up. The branches beneath the tree house began to sway. And the tree house creaked and groaned. A blast of thunder made the tree shake. They all screamed in terror.

"They talked about going home. But the rain was coming down hard now. They decided to wait out the storm. Strong storms like these never lasted long, they thought.

"And then it happened.

"A lightning bolt shattered the clouds. It sliced

through the heavy treetops and pierced the tree house.

"The tree house burst into flames."

Betsy swallowed hard.

Lightning. That made sense. I remembered the charred black boards in the lower platform.

"The kids were up on the top platform," Betsy continued. "They couldn't escape. The horrible flames leaped up in front of them. Behind them.

"Thick black smoke billowed everywhere.

"They cried out for help—but it was too late."

"Some people say you can still hear their terrifying screams on rainy nights," Kate whispered.

I stared over at the tree house. I pictured it in flames. I imagined the cries. The horrible cries for help. I shuddered.

"So that's it?" Steve asked. "That's why we shouldn't build the tree house? We're not dumb enough to stay in a tree house in a thunderstorm."

"That's not why," I said. I understood what Betsy was trying to tell us. "The tree house is haunted now, right? It's haunted by the ghosts of the kids."

Betsy nodded. Then she went on.

"Many years after the accident, some kids tried to rebuild the tree house. But they didn't have time to finish it. . . ."

"What happened to them?" I whispered. I could feel my heart pounding in my chest as Betsy continued.

"No one knows the whole story. At first, little things went wrong. One of the boys fell off the ladder—a rung broke."

"Big deal," Steve interrupted. "The wood was probably old—so it broke."

Betsy continued. "But it wasn't an old rung—it was one of the new ones they had just fixed. Another kid came down with a strange fever. It turned out he had like a million spider bites."

Spider bites.

I could feel the spiderwebs on my face as she talked.

"Then things got really strange. No matter how hard they worked—the tree house was never finished. Boards that were hammered in one day were found on the ground the next day.

"Finally the kids realized the tree house was haunted. They stopped working on it—all except for one kid. I think his name was Duncan."

"What happened to Duncan?" Steve asked.

"He kept working on the tree house. Until . . . until one day his brother found him. He was lying under the tree house. A hammer had fallen and knocked him out."

"Was he dead?" I managed to croak.

"No one knows," Kate said. "His family moved away after that. And no one has dared to go near the tree house since then."

I glanced around the woods. Nothing moved. Everything was silent. So silent I could hear Kate's soft breathing across from me.

"Now you know why you can't work on the tree house," Kate said. "We probably shouldn't even be in this clearing. We're too close. Much too close."

"You're right," Betsy said. "Let's get out of here. This place is giving me the creeps."

"Are you going?" Kate asked.

I didn't answer. There were too many thoughts racing around in my brain. The webs . . . The hammer . . . That kid Duncan . . . The haunted tree house . . .

"We've got some stuff to do," I finally answered. "We'll see you around."

Betsy gave me a long, hard stare. "I don't think you're going to be around much longer," she said. "Not if you stay here."

Then she grabbed Kate's arm and they ran across the clearing and disappeared into the woods.

"Those girls are seriously weird," Steve said. "Even weirder than you, Dylan. They're really scared some ghost is going to swoop down and grab them."

"You don't think that story is true?" I asked.

47

"Of course not," Steve shot back. "Ghosts don't exist, Dylan, my lad. Trust me. I'm older. I know more than you do."

Yeah, right, I thought. "Then how did that story get started? And what happened to the hammer in the middle of the platform? How come it fell on me?"

Steve groaned.

"I'll tell you how come that hammer fell," I said to Steve. "The ghost threw it at me—as a warning!"

9

I managed to trick, bargain, or bribe Steve into working on the tree house every day until Friday. On Fridays Steve has band practice. He smashes cymbals together once or twice during a concert— then he brags about what a great musician he is.

So I had to go out to the tree house alone. *This probably isn't such a good idea,* I thought as I walked through the woods. The ghost Kate and Betsy had described didn't exactly sound friendly. But if there was a ghost out there, I wanted to see it, I decided. No matter what.

I thought about the girls' story—the broken rung on the ladder. The spider bites. The hammer.

The hammer. A shiver ran through me. I sure

was luckier than that boy Duncan. But would my luck hold out?

The clearing was just up ahead.

I walked a few steps into it and stopped.

"Oh, no!" I groaned.

All our boards and nails—all of them—had been destroyed.

They lay scattered everywhere—all over the clearing, between the trees—everywhere. I even spotted some boards on the ground deep in the forest.

They were all bent and twisted. Deformed.

I swallowed hard and stared up at the dark windows of the tree house. Nothing moved inside.

I slowly crossed the clearing.

I glanced up at the tree house before each step.

I was terrified—terrified that the ghost was getting ready to swoop down on me.

I reached the base of the old oak and stood there. Waiting. Waiting for something to happen.

Nothing did.

So I began cleaning up the mess, nervously checking over my shoulder every few minutes.

It would take me hours to find all the nails and clean up this mess. Now I was more angry than scared.

"It's going to take more than this to stop me!" I yelled out. "I'm not like those other kids!"

When I stopped screaming the woods felt quieter than ever. Spookier.

That's right, Dylan, I thought. *Invite the ghost to come out and pound you. Very smart.*

I glanced around. Nothing moved.

I grabbed one of the cardboard boxes and began tossing nails into it. Nails that I had straightened out. This was going to take forever.

At this moment the only one I hated more than the ghost was Steve. How come he always manages to be busy when I need him the most?

After I had gathered up all the nails I could find, I began collecting the boards. I stacked up the ones in the clearing first. Then I gathered the others that had been tossed in the woods.

As I hauled the last one back to the clearing, I peered up at the tree house—and spotted something high on the trunk.

I wasn't sure what it was. I walked a few steps closer and squinted.

Claw marks.

It looked like claw marks.

Huge, black claw marks.

I'd never seen an animal with claws big enough to make those marks. And I wasn't even sure a big animal could get way up there.

But there was one thing I *was* sure about—those marks weren't there yesterday.

I moved closer to the tree and stared hard. That's when I realized I wasn't staring at claw marks.

I was looking at something worse. Much worse.

They were letters. Letters burned into the trunk of the tree.

My heart pounded as I spelled out the message. S-T-A-Y-A-W-A-Y.

Stay away!

10

"**G**et real, Dylan," Steve said. "For the hundredth time, there are no ghosts. Not here. Not in the tree house. Not anywhere."

"What about the letters?" I spat back.

"Well, Dylan, my lad. I have a theory about those letters. I think you put them there," he said, "to make me believe in ghosts. It was a nice try—but it's not going to work."

I wanted to strangle Steve.

But I made a suggestion instead.

"We can settle our ghost argument once and for all tonight," I told him.

"Why? What happens tonight?" he asked.

"Tonight we are going to sleep out in the woods. And we are going to finally meet a ghost."

It took the usual arguments before Steve agreed to sleep outside with me that night.

"You want me to camp out in the freezing cold— without any TV? Are you crazy?" he hollered.

"You're not afraid, are you?" I challenged.

"How can I be afraid of something that doesn't exist?" Steve snapped. "You're the one who's always getting spooked. I'm just not doing it—that's all."

"Do you still have that book report to write for your English class?" I asked.

And that was the end of that. Steve and I were going to sleep out.

"The deal was that I sleep out with you tonight," Steve said as he squirmed his way into his sleeping bag. "That means I sleep. You watch."

"How am I going to prove ghosts exist if I can't wake you up when one appears?" I argued.

"It's not going to happen, Dylan," he answered. He closed his eyes and rolled over on his side. "But if it does, if by some miracle you're right and I'm wrong and you find a ghost—you can wake me up. But you'd better be absolutely sure it's a ghost. Or I'll pound you."

54

My brother is such an idiot, I thought. But it's better to be out in the woods with an idiot than with no one at all.

I didn't plan to sleep. So I sat cross-legged on my sleeping bag, with my flashlight, camera, and tape recorder all ready to go.

I also had a thermometer so I'd know how cold the ghost made the air. And a compass—to study its effect on the earth's magnetic field.

I even put a plate of cookies and crackers and Cheese Curlies at the bottom of the oak tree. I'd always wondered if ghosts ate. None of my books mentioned food. But I wanted to be prepared for anything.

I was ready.

I pressed the record button on the tape recorder. "Testing one, two. Testing. This is Dylan S. Brown," I whispered into it. It is Friday, April 21st, 10:38 P.M. My assistant, Steve Brown, and I successfully sneaked out of the house.

"We have set up a base camp in the Fear Street Woods, near the clearing next to the tree house. I hope the trees will hide us from the ghost. I want to observe it before I decide to make contact. It is too dark to photograph the words I discovered burned into the tree trunk. I will document them tomorrow."

Steve gave a little half-snort, half-snore. "My assistant has fallen asleep," I continued. "More later." I clicked off the tape recorder.

I raised my binoculars and studied the tree house.

No lights.

No movement.

Nothing staring back at me.

I let the binoculars fall back around my neck.

Then I heard a rustling sound. Not very loud— but coming from the direction of the tree house.

Something was definitely out there.

I thought about waking Steve up. But I didn't. I wasn't sure yet if it was the ghost. And if it wasn't, he'd kill me.

I picked up my binoculars and pressed them to my face.

I peered into the darkness.

I couldn't see a thing.

Should I turn on my flashlight? I wanted to, but if I did whatever was out there would see me. And I didn't want to scare it off.

I listened hard. There it was again. That same rustling sound. Even though I was wearing my blue winter parka, I shivered. The air around me felt colder now.

I checked the thermometer. Five degrees cooler than before. I knew it!

56

My pulse began to race. Chills ran up and down my spine.

I should be taping this, I thought. With a shaky hand I punched on the record button.

Should I wake Steve up now?

No. Not yet. I needed more proof.

The noise again. Louder this time.

Part of me wanted to duck down into my sleeping bag and zip it over my head. But I couldn't. I had to get closer. I had to see my ghost.

I picked up the flashlight and crawled away from my sleeping bag. I dodged behind the closest tree. The noise continued. The ghost didn't spot me.

I stayed low to the ground—on my hands and knees.

Crawling from tree to tree.

Crawling closer to the old oak.

My heart pounded so hard I thought it would burst out of my chest.

But now I was there. Behind a large rock right next to the old oak.

I peeked out from behind my hiding spot. Too dark. I still couldn't see anything. But I could hear it.

I steadied my flashlight in my trembling hand. I held it straight out in front of me. I flipped it on.

Two cold, dark eyes were caught in its beam.

A cat.

A gray cat eating Cheese Curlies.

I let out the longest sigh of my life.

Beads of sweat dripped from my forehead. I sank back against the tree and wiped them off.

Creak.

I jerked my head back toward the old oak.

Creak.

The cat darted into the woods.

Creak.

I recognized that sound—the sound of someone walking on the old wooden boards of the tree house.

Creak. Creak.

This is it, I thought. This is really it. I stood up and inched closer to the tree house.

I held my breath. I was afraid to breathe. Afraid the ghost would hear me.

I stood a foot away from the tree house. I squinted up into the darkness.

One of the boards on the wall of the tree house moved . . . as if someone up there was shaking it.

I heard the sound of nails—nails squealing as they were pried loose.

Then *pop!* I saw the board flip up. And suddenly, as I watched, it came hurtling through the air.

"Steve!" I shrieked. "Steve! It's the ghost. It's the ghost. It's tearing apart our tree house!"

CRASH!

The board hit the ground a few feet from me.

Ping ping ping.

Nails flew through the air, bouncing off the branches of the surrounding trees.

I raced over to Steve. I shook him hard. "Get up!" I screamed. "Get up!"

"What?" he muttered, rubbing his eyes.

Creak!

"Run!" I yelled. "Run! It's coming after us."

Another board came soaring out of the tree house.

THUD!

It hit the ground right next to my sleeping bag.

I tore down the path. Steve was right behind me. We had to get home before the ghost grabbed us.

I couldn't see where I was going. But I didn't slow down.

A tree branch slashed across my face. A trickle of blood dripped down my cheek. I kept running. My lungs burned. I gasped for air.

My aching legs cried out for me to stop. But I couldn't stop. Not now.

I burst into the backyard.

Did Steve make it?

I spun around to check.

He almost ran right into me. "What did you—" he began.

Then his mouth dropped open. He was staring at something over my shoulder. "Oh, no," he whispered.

Then I felt it. Something big, cold, and clammy clutching the back of my shirt.

It grabbed the back of my neck and pulled me across the wet grass!

12

My knees buckled underneath me. I began to sink to the ground.

"Let me go!" I screamed. "I promise I'll stay away from your tree house!" But the ghost raised me up.

"What are you doing out here?"

Dad.

"We were camping out to catch a ghost," I explained in a rush. "It came after us. We almost didn't get away in time."

"What's going on out there?" Mom stood under the back door light. I could see her tighten the belt on her old pink robe.

"In the house," Dad ordered us. "Dylan and

Steve were hunting ghosts in the woods," he explained to Mom.

She held the door open for us. "How could you go out this late at night?" she asked, really angry.

"Why were you running?" Dad asked. "What happened?"

"Nothing happened," Steve muttered. He sounded totally calm.

"Nothing happened?" I squeaked. "The ghost—"

"It's late," Dad interrupted. "You two get to bed. We'll discuss this in the morning."

Steve and I slunk up the stairs to our room. "What do you mean nothing happened?" I demanded the second Steve shut the door behind us.

"I mean nothing happened," Steve answered. "You got scared and ran back here. I came after you."

"Oh, right!" I cried. "You were scared, too."

"No, I wasn't," Steve replied. "There was nothing to be scared of."

"What about the board? You saw the board crash to the ground."

"Oh, that's a really big deal," Steve said, laughing. "A board from an old wrecked tree house fell down. A tree house that's falling apart. What a shock!"

"It wasn't just one board," I protested. "And it

62

didn't just come loose. The ghost pried it loose. It's just like what happened to the kids Betsy told us about. The ghost doesn't want us to finish the tree house—so he's taking it apart."

"Listen to me," Steve replied. "I'm older. I know more than you do. And there are no such things as ghosts, Dylan. No ghosts! No ghosts!"

"You don't know that for sure."

Steve jumped off his bed. He pulled a pair of high-tops out of the closet and pulled them on. "You are driving me insane. We're going back to the tree house. Right now."

"What?"

"You heard me." Steve pulled on a red sweatshirt over the one he already wore. "We're settling this ghost thing tonight. We're going to check out the tree house. And you're going to admit that there's no such things as ghosts."

Steve opened our door. "Come on," he whispered.

I didn't move.

I didn't need any more proof of ghosts. And I didn't care what Steve thought.

I had seen enough.

Ghosts were real.

And scary.

"Dylan! Let's go."

I shook my head no.

"Aha! So you admit it!" he cried.

Half of me wanted to jump in bed and never come out. The other half wanted to strangle Steve.

I had no choice. I crept down the stairs after my brother.

"Ssstop," Steve hissed when we were almost to the kitchen door. "Mom and Dad are in there."

We froze. "I'm worried about Dylan," Mom said. "All he talks about is ghosts. He has no other interests."

"You should have seen him in the backyard. He looked terrified. Maybe tonight was enough to convince him to give up," Dad replied.

"I hope so," Mom answered. "Why don't you go up and check on them."

"Go!" Steve whispered. He pushed me toward the stairs.

We flew up to our room. Steve eased our door shut. I scrambled into the top bunk and pulled up the covers.

I heard Dad coming up the stairs. Oh, no! We left the light on. Too late to do anything about it.

I squeezed my eyes shut and tried to breathe deeply.

Our door opened. "Must be even more scared than I thought," Dad muttered. "They left the light on."

That's when I realized my right foot was sticking out of the covers.

And I still had my shoes on. If Dad noticed my sneaker, it was over.

Dad stood in the doorway for a long moment. Should I pull my foot in? Or would that draw attention to it?

I knew I'd never be able to come up with a good excuse for going to bed with my shoes on.

Dad took a step into the room.

My eye started to twitch. A nervous twitch.

I waited . . . and heard Dad snap off the light and shut our door.

Yes!

"Let's wait about an hour for Mom and Dad to go to sleep," Steve whispered. "Then we're going back out there. Because this is the last night you'll ever say the word *ghost* again!"

An hour later I was staring up at the tree house.

"Keep going," Steve ordered. "We're checking out every inch of it." He shoved me toward the rungs.

I didn't hear any creaks. Or any squealing nails. *That's a good sign,* I told myself. The ghost probably left.

But a tiny movement in the far corner of the

65

second level caught my eye. Then I saw a shadowy form move down to the first floor.

I dug my fingers into Steve's arm.

"Ow!" Steve complained.

"Do you see it?" I whispered. "Look!"

Steve peered up.

His eyes were glued to the tree house.

To the ghost who was waiting there.

13

"**I** don't see anything," Steve declared. "Now climb up."

"The ghost is there," I insisted. "It just moved down to the bottom platform."

"Great. I can't wait to meet it," Steve said. He gave me a hard shove.

"We can't just go barging up there," I whispered. "We don't want to make it angry. Remember what happened to that boy Duncan."

Duncan. Dylan. Even our names sounded alike. I couldn't help thinking I was going to be the next ghost of Fear Street.

"Yoohoo! Mr. Ghost, we're coming to visit," Steve whispered.

He thinks he's so funny. "You go first, since you think it's all such a big joke."

"Nope. This is your ghost."

I climbed the first rung of the ladder. Steve stood right behind me.

My mouth felt totally dry. I tried to swallow, but I couldn't.

Steve poked me in the back. "Come on," he said. "It's cold here. I'm freezing."

I climbed onto the second rung. Only three more to go. *You* want *to see a ghost,* I reminded myself. *But I'd rather see it from farther away,* I added.

Steve poked me again.

I felt around for the third rung of the ladder. Then I remembered. The old board was rotten and I hadn't hammered the new one on yet.

I reached up and grabbed the fifth rung.

Then my fingers slipped. And I crashed to the ground, taking Steve with me.

I moaned as the back of my head hit a rock. I tried to lift my head, but I felt too dizzy.

I slowly opened my eyes.

And saw *two* pale faces hovering above me.

Their eyes gleamed.

Their mouths hung open wide.

Ghosts! *Two* ghosts!

Their hands stretched toward me.

Reaching. Reaching.

"Stay away!" I shrieked.

Steve saw them, too. "Run, Dylan!" he cried. "Run!"

14

Two ghosts. How could there be two ghosts?

I struggled to my feet.

"Stay away!" I shrieked.

"Don't hurt me, please," Steve cried.

"Please leave us alone!" I begged.

"Ooooooh! Ooooooh!" one of the ghosts moaned.

"Please. Please," one ghost mocked.

"Don't hurt me, please," the other one chanted.

Then they started to giggle.

They didn't cackle or howl like ghosts. They giggled like girls.

Human girls.

Betsy and Kate.

They were stretched out on their stomachs with their heads hanging out the trapdoor.

"Please leave us alone!" Betsy laughed until she choked.

And here's the worst part. Steve was laughing, too.

"Ooooh, a ghost, I'm *sooo* scared," Steve said.

I felt my face burn. My hands clenched into fists. "You think this is funny?" I demanded. "You are all sick."

Kate clambered down the ladder. Betsy followed right behind her.

"You-you're the ones who have been playing all those tricks?" I stammered. "The hammer? The boards? Everything?"

"Well, yes," Betsy admitted. "You wouldn't listen to me when I tried to tell you the tree house was haunted. So we decided to haunt it ourselves."

No ghosts. Just dumb girls teasing me. It's the story of my life. I'm never going to see a real ghost. Never.

"We really fooled you, didn't we?" Kate exclaimed. She bounced up and down, her ponytail flying.

"I know you believed every word of my ghost story," Betsy chimed in.

"No, I didn't," I protested. "I wanted to keep an

open mind. Lots of scientists believe in ghosts, and—"

"Don't lie," Steve interrupted. "Admit it. They got you good."

"We spent half the day setting up that barricade around the tree," Betsy explained. "Good thing we're on vacation. Being ghosts is hard work."

Steve started to laugh again. "I told Dylan a million times there are no such things as ghosts. But does he listen to his older—"

"Shut up!" I yelled. "All of you. Just shut up."

"Don't be angry," Kate pleaded. "We knew you wanted to see a ghost . . . and so . . . and so . . ." She ruined her apology by bursting into giggles again.

"Come on, Dylan, my lad," Steve said in that big brother voice I hate. "I'll take you home. You've had quite a scare."

"Me! What about you? You screamed when you saw them, remember?" I was so mad I could barely get the words out.

"I did not scream. Like I always say, Dylan— there are no ghosts. Now let's go home. It's way past your bedtime."

Steve and I took off across the clearing. Kate and Betsy kept calling for us to come back. But no way. I couldn't face them.

I felt like a total jerk. I couldn't speak.

I just headed toward home with Steve.

As soon as we were through the clearing and hidden by the woods, Steve stopped and grabbed my arm. "I'm going to kill you, Dylan. You made us look like morons."

I jerked my arm away and shoved him. "How did I make you look like a moron?" I snapped. "You laughed your head off."

"Yeah, but thanks to you I was out there sneaking around looking for *ghosts.*"

"You're always telling me how much smarter you are. Why did you bother listening to me?" I asked.

That shut him up.

We walked the rest of the way back in silence. When we reached the house, Steve opened the door and said, "You're right. I'm never listening to you again."

We stepped into the kitchen. Steve leaned close to me and whispered, "Wake up Mom and Dad and you're dead meat."

"I'm sooo scared," I whispered back.

We crept through the kitchen and up the stairs to our room. I kicked off my shoes without bothering to untie them. Mom hates that, but I was too tired to care.

I climbed straight into bed.

But I couldn't fall asleep.

I kept hearing Kate and Betsy.

Giggling.

I hate them, I thought. *I really, really hate them.*

I rolled over onto my side. Then I tried my back. Then the other side. I couldn't get comfortable.

"Stop moving around up there," Steve grumbled. "I'm trying to sleep."

"I'm trying to sleep, too." Then I rolled over and made the bed shake as much as I could.

Steve growled.

I closed my eyes. And thought.

Then I bolted up in bed.

I know what would make me feel better!

I was going to get even with Betsy and Kate.

I was going to give them the worst scare of their lives.

Now I just had to figure out how.

15

The next day started out bad. And then got worse. Steve woke me up at five A.M. because it was raining. I had to deliver his newspapers when it rained. That was the deal.

The papers weighed a ton. I couldn't throw them on a porch from the curb. So I had to get off my bike at every house and run the paper to the door. In the rain.

When I returned home, Dad handed me a list of chores that he wanted Steve and me to do. A list a mile long. They would take the rest of the day—at least.

"After you finish these," he said, "you should be

pretty tired. Too tired to sneak out in the middle of the night."

Ha-ha, Dad.

Before I started chore number one—clean the garage—I wanted a bowl of Froot Loops. They're my favorite cereal. But the box was empty.

I knew Steve ate the last bowl—Mom and Dad hate Froot Loops. So does Steve. But he finished them because today was get-even-with-Dylan-day—for making him look like an idiot in front of the girls.

I headed out to the garage—wet *and* hungry. I was in a really bad mood now.

I found Steve reading a comic book. Of course he hadn't started the chores without me. I asked him why.

"Why should I," he said, "when everything was your fault?"

How did I make it through the morning without killing Steve? By imagining ways to get even with Betsy and Kate. As I sorted and stacked rolls of duct tape, electrical tape, and masking tape, I pictured myself taping Kate and Betsy's mouths shut.

That way they would never be able to fool anyone again with their stupid stories.

As I organized the paint cans along one wall, I imagined dumping paint over their heads, turning their black hair green or orange. Or green *and* orange.

By the time we had cleaned the whole garage, I'd come up with about a thousand awful things to do to them.

But none of them were right.

None of them were scary enough.

In the late afternoon, after all my chores were done, I decided to visit the tree house. Just one last time, I told myself.

I wasn't afraid of meeting a ghost anymore. Not there, anyway. I still believed in ghosts—don't get me wrong. But I didn't think the tree house was haunted—except by two stupid girls.

I circled the old oak, studying the work Steve and I had done. The tree house was coming out great. The first floor was complete, and we had begun work on the second level.

I found one of the boards that Betsy and Kate had pried loose. It was lying on the grass next to one of my cardboard boxes.

I brushed the dirt off it and picked up my hammer. Then I climbed up into the tree house and hammered it back into place.

I went back down for some more boards. I had trouble getting them up into the tree by myself, but somehow I managed.

Before I knew it, it was time for dinner—and I had built two entire walls!

"I'm going to finish this tree house," I muttered. "Even if I have to do it all by myself."

The tree house will be great when it's done, I thought as I made my way back home. *And those stupid girls will be really jealous. Because I won't let them anywhere near it.*

That night I sat on my bed and stared out the window. Still plotting my revenge.

That's when I spotted the lights. Lights coming from the direction of the tree house.

"You're not going to believe this, Steve!" I exclaimed.

"I'm not listening to you," Steve informed me, without bothering to look up from his comic book.

"Oh," I said. "So you aren't interested in the fact that the girls are back out by the tree house?"

Steve jumped up and charged over to the window. "I can't believe them!" he cried. "Even you aren't dumb enough to fall for their dumb trick two nights in a row."

That's when I came up with my idea.

The perfect idea for revenge.

"No, tonight they are going to fall for one of *our* tricks," I told Steve. "Put on a black shirt, black pants, black everything."

"How about a black eye for you?" my very mature brother replied. "Now leave me alone."

"Please, Steve," I begged. "You have to come with me. Just one last time. To get even with those girls."

Steve glanced out the window again. I could tell he was going to change his mind.

"What's the plan?" he asked.

"Tonight *we'll* be the ghosts of the tree house," I explained. "We'll sneak up on them and scare them to death!"

Steve smiled. He grabbed his black sweatshirt and pulled it over his head. "We'll scare them good."

In a few minutes we were both dressed in black. Steve even found a black baseball cap. We crept downstairs and into the backyard. We decided not to risk using flashlights.

We moved along the path slowly. We didn't want to make a sound. We wanted to surprise them.

It seemed as if it took forever but we finally reached the clearing.

Please let them still be there, I thought. *Please. Please. Please.*

I peered up at the tree house. And spotted a light on the first level.

Yes!

As we tiptoed closer to the tree house, every

sound thundered in my ears. My sneakers squeaking on the wet grass. Steve's breathing. My heart pounding.

Don't let them hear us, I thought. *Not now. Not when we're so close.*

We made it to the big rock next to the old oak and ducked behind it. I motioned to Steve that I would go up the ladder first. He'd follow right behind.

I carefully climbed the ladder. I made sure I had my weight balanced and my hands positioned on each rung before I took the next step. We were so close to success—I didn't want to ruin everything now.

One rung. Two. Three. Four. Only one more to go.

I climbed to the fifth rung.

I carefully reached up to the trapdoor.

I made sure I had a firm grip on it.

I glanced down to make sure Steve was in position behind me.

Then I flung open the door. And burst into the tree house with a loud howl.

But what I saw made me scream in terror.

I thought I would scream forever.

80

16

A ghost.

A real ghost.

It looked like a boy. A boy about my age. But I could see right through him.

As I leaped up through the trapdoor, he reached out to grab me. His icy fingers brushed my cheek.

I dodged his grasp and flung myself against the wall.

And then Steve jumped up into the tree house, howling his special werewolf howl. It turned into a whine when he spotted the ghost.

The ghost extended both his arms straight out. His hands were clenched in tight fists. I watched in horror as he slowly uncurled his fingers and pointed them at Steve.

A gust of icy wind blew up—up from the ghost's hands. It swept Steve off his feet and sent him *whooshing* toward me.

Then there was a loud *thud!* The thud of the trapdoor slamming shut.

Steve and I huddled together in the corner. I was sweating even though the room was freezing cold. Beads of sweat dripped down my forehead and into my eyes. I wanted to blink. But I didn't dare.

I didn't dare take my eyes off the ghost.

The ghost started to move toward us. He seemed to walk, but his feet never really touched the floor.

His eyes—his glowing red eyes—stared into mine. I lifted my hand to wipe the sweat from my forehead. The ghost's eyes flickered. I dropped my hand down to my side—fast.

I could feel Steve trembling beside me. "Wh-what do you think he's going to do?" he whispered.

I didn't answer. I couldn't. All I could do was stare. Stare into those terrifying eyes.

The ghost moved closer.

Closer.

He lifted his filmy white arms and began to reach out. Reach out for us.

His lips parted in an evil sneer.

The air around us grew colder. My teeth began to chatter.

Closer. Closer.

He was inches from us now.

Do something, do something, I told myself. Don't just stand there. *DO SOMETHING!*

I leaped around the ghost and lunged across the room. Across to the trapdoor.

I slid on my stomach and grabbed for the handle. I began to pull, but it slipped out of my sweaty hand.

The ghost howled in fury. He rose up in the air.

I scrambled up on my knees and grabbed the handle again.

"Hurry, Dylan!" Steve screamed. "Hurry!"

The ghost swooped down.

I jerked the door open.

The ghost flew right at me. Then he flew right through me. He hovered over my head. I froze in sheer terror.

I stared up into his eyes. They glowed an angry red.

He floated close to me. I could feel his icy breath on my neck. Then he reached down and banged the trapdoor hard. It slammed shut.

"Don't move," he howled. "You're not going anywhere ever again."

17

"**Y**ou're not going anywhere ever again," the ghost repeated. "I can't let you leave. Not yet."

I shot a glance at Steve, but he sat shriveled up in the corner. His mouth gaped open and his hands and legs trembled. *He's not going to be much help here,* I thought.

"What do you want?" I managed to ask.

"I need your help," the ghost said.

"Help? What help? Who are you?" I was actually talking to a ghost!

He looked just like a regular kid. A regular kid I could see right through.

"My name is Corey—or it was Corey when I was alive. . . ." the ghost replied softly.

When I was alive.

"So you're really a ghost," I said to Corey—but I was staring at Steve.

"How does it feel to be a ghost?" I blurted out. I had so many questions. Now was my chance to get some answers. Especially since the ghost wasn't letting us go anywhere.

"I guess it feels like being asleep," he began to explain. "I'm not exactly sure. You see, this is my first day as a ghost. Before this I was trapped in this tree house—without any shape at all. But you changed all that."

"I-I did?" I asked.

"Yes," the ghost replied. "The more you worked on the tree house, the stronger I grew. Now I can move around. I can see again. I haven't been able to do that since I died. And I have a voice and a body—well, sort of a body. But I still can't leave the tree house. I'm still too weak."

"H-how did you become a ghost?" I asked.

"I died in this tree house," he replied. "In a lightning storm."

"Wow! Steve, did you hear that? The story is true," I cried.

Steve didn't say anything. To tell you the truth, I think he was in shock.

But I wasn't afraid at all. The ghost didn't seem scary. He just seemed sad. Sad and lonely.

"You said you need our help," I whispered. "What do you want us to do?"

"I want you to finish building the tree house," the ghost explained. "I've been trapped in this tree house where I died—for years and years. But if you finish the tree house, I'm sure I'll be strong enough to leave here."

That's all? That's easy! It's almost finished anyway, I thought.

"Will you help me?" the ghost asked again.

"Yeah. We'll help you," Steve interrupted before I could answer. "But we want to make a deal."

"A deal?" The ghost boy's voice sounded cold and hard. He floated over to Steve—and seeing him hover in the air made my body clench with fear.

"Why should I make a deal with *you?*" he bellowed.

18

I couldn't believe it! I'd been doing all the talking while my very mature brother hid in the corner. And now he wanted to make a deal!

Steve's going to ruin everything. We'll never get out of here alive.

I glared at Steve. "We don't have to make—"

Steve cut me off again. "We'll help you on one condition," he declared. "You have to help us get even with two girls."

"And you'll finish the tree house—no delays?" the ghost said.

"Yes," I said eagerly.

"Then I will help you," the ghost said.

"Deal," Steve replied. "Now here's the plan. . . ."

The next week Steve and I worked every day after school on the tree house.

Steve didn't read one comic book.

He didn't make one trip back to the house for Cheese Curlies.

I didn't even have to bribe him with doughnuts.

And now it was Saturday—and we were just about finished. The tree house looked awesome.

"Steve, I need some more nails," I called from the roof.

"Here, Dylan. Catch!" Steve threw a handful of nails at me. They flew over the roof and landed on the ground. Steve was turning back into his old self.

"Why do you have to act like such a jerk?" I shouted.

"Dylan, my lad, I can't wait until we're finished with the tree house. Then I'll never have to see you again."

"We still share a room," I replied.

"Not for long," Steve answered.

"Why?" I asked. "Are you going somewhere?"

"Nope," Steve answered. "You are."

"I don't think so, Steve."

"Oh, yes, you are. It's part of the deal I made with the ghost. You're moving into the tree house.

Corey needs someone to take over haunting the tree house. I told him you would do it. You like ghosts so much, I figured you wouldn't mind becoming one."

"How could you do this to me?" I yelled. "I'm not doing it!"

"A deal's a deal, Dylan, my lad," Steve answered. Then he started to laugh. "Boy, you'll believe anything!"

I was ready to throw my hammer at Steve, but I stopped when I heard voices down below.

Girls' voices.

Betsy and Kate.

"They're here," I whispered to Steve.

"I knew they would show up," Steve whispered back.

"Wow!" Kate said as she and Betsy approached the old oak. "The tree house is almost finished."

"Yeah. Your dumb tricks didn't work," I mumbled under my breath.

Kate and Betsy walked around the tree house slowly, studying it. "It looks really good," Kate finally said. "I'll bet this is what it looked like when it was first built."

Betsy nodded. "It's not bad," she said. "But you're lucky you didn't get hurt."

I opened my mouth to start to tell them off. But Kate cut me off.

"Maybe those terrible stories we heard weren't true. Maybe someone was trying to trick us," she said.

Yeah. Sure. Right, I thought.

"Listen," Steve said. "Why don't the four of us try to be friends from now on? We're going to have a party up here tonight. To celebrate finishing the tree house. Want to come?"

Kate and Betsy didn't answer right away. Kate started nibbling on her ponytail.

"Sure," Betsy finally agreed.

"Great," Steve said. "We'll meet here after dark. It'll be fun!"

The girls left.

Steve and I finished hammering in the last nails on the tree house roof. Then we climbed down and inspected our work from every angle.

The tree house looked really awesome!

We dashed home, gulped down dinner, and collected stuff for the party—chips, soda, things like that.

As soon as it grew dark out, we headed back through the woods. I had gotten used to it being so quiet out here. The Fear Street Woods didn't frighten me anymore.

Steve and I climbed the ladder and set out everything for the party.

Steve popped a Cheese Curlie in his mouth and

walked over to the tree house window. "Here they come!" he whispered.

We could hear the girls climbing the ladder. Steve pulled open the trapdoor for them. "Come on in," he called.

Betsy peeked her head through the door first. Kate was right behind her.

"What do you think?" I asked as they glanced around the first level.

Betsy remained silent. Kate's eyes looked as if they were about to pop right out of her head. "Wow! It really turned out great," she finally said.

The girls plopped down on the floor. I started to pour soda for everyone.

And that's when we heard it.

A soft moan.

"Wh-what was that?" Kate asked.

"Probably just the wind," Steve replied.

Then we heard it again.

Louder this time. And creepier. Almost like a wail.

Betsy grabbed Kate's hand. "We're leaving," she declared.

She moved to the trapdoor, bent down, and grasped its handle.

But before she could pull it open, an icy wind blew through the tree house, sending everything soaring through the air.

The chips whirled around the room. Cups of soda flew up and splattered against the wall.

Steve and I braced ourselves on the floor.

Betsy's knuckles turned white as she gripped the trapdoor handle. Her eyes were wide with fright.

And then Corey sprang up—right through the trapdoor. He let out the most hideous shriek I've ever heard.

The girls screamed their heads off.

Corey stretched himself to twice his normal size. He really was much stronger—now that we'd finished the house for him.

He swung his filmy arms wildly and the icy wind blew stronger. His eyes glowed like red embers. And his mouth gaped open—showing rows and rows of rotted, black teeth.

Steve laughed like a maniac. His plan had worked—the girls were getting the worst scare of their lives.

I stared at the girls as they shrieked and shrieked. They couldn't stop.

And then I saw something.

Something that made my breath catch in my throat.

Something that made my heart stop.

19

Betsy and Kate rose up in the air.

Up to join Corey.

As I watched, the color faded from their bodies. Their black hair turned a misty white. Their eyes began to glow a deep red.

My heart pounded. I thought my chest was going to explode.

The girls wrapped their arms around Corey. And they hugged!

"They're ghosts, too!" I howled. "They're ghosts, too!"

Steve raised his eyes to the weird scene. I heard him give a low groan.

The three ghosts cackled and danced in the air. They spun around and around.

Cold air shot through me as they flew past. My teeth started to chatter.

"Run!" Steve screamed. "Run!"

I flung open the trapdoor.

As we slid down the trunk I could feel my skin ripping open against the rough bark. It didn't matter. Nothing mattered except getting away— fast.

We bolted across the clearing toward the woods.

We nearly reached the path.

And then the ghosts swooped down on us.

They joined hands and surrounded us. Surrounded us in an icy circle of air.

My whole body trembled as the ghosts whirled around us. Faster and faster. And laughing—evil, hideous laughs.

Corey swung in front of me and grinned in triumph.

And then the ghosts began to move in.

Closer and closer.

Tightening the circle.

Until we were trapped.

20

~~~

"We have to get out of here—now!" I screamed to Steve.

Steve and I flung ourselves at the ghosts. But the ghosts bounced us right back. Back to the center of the circle.

I tried again. I flew at the filmy creatures with all my might.

This time they caught me. I was stuck right between two quivering, icy ghosts. I felt as if I were being smothered in freezing-cold Jell-O.

I started to shiver. My arms and legs shook and my teeth chattered. My lips began to turn numb.

I couldn't breathe. I started to choke. I was freezing. Freezing to death.

It was all a trick, I thought. A horrible trick. Corey made us finish the tree house. And now he's going to kill us.

Steve sank to the ground and curled up in a little ball. I clenched my fists and threw myself against the ghosts. I pushed and pushed. Then with one last burst of strength, I shoved against them hard.

I was out! I doubled over, gulping down air. I could breathe again. And I was free!

I straightened up—and that's when I realized the awful truth. I was still inside the circle.

"You can't keep me here!" I screamed, running forward again—pushing against the clammy cold that surrounded me.

Betsy shrieked with laughter. Corey laughed, too.

"Stop! Stop! Can't you see they're scared?" It was Kate.

The laughter died.

Then Betsy spoke.

"I'm sorry," she said. "We were just playing. We didn't mean to scare you."

"Yeah," Corey added. "I guess we got carried away."

Carried away? This must be a bad dream, I thought. A really bad dream.

"Corey is our brother," Kate began. "We thought we would never find him."

My mouth dropped open.

I glanced at Steve. He sat shriveled up on the ground, staring into space.

"Corey, Betsy, and I were the three kids in the tree house—the kids we told you about," Kate continued. "When the tree house was hit by lightning, Betsy and I were on one side of it. Corey was on the other side."

"We all died at the same time," Betsy said, taking up the story. "When we became ghosts, Kate and I were together. But Corey disappeared. His spirit was lost. We've been searching for him ever since."

Kate waited for me to say something. But I didn't. I was afraid to speak. I was afraid to move. I was too afraid to do anything but listen.

"When you discovered the tree house," she went on, "we suddenly found ourselves back in these woods. We *thought* we had been brought back to scare you away from it. So you wouldn't get hurt—the way we did."

"But now we know we were wrong," Betsy interrupted. "We must have been brought back to find Corey. And you two helped us!"

"Thank you. Thank you so much," Corey added. "You freed me from the tree house. Finally!"

"Yes!" Betsy exclaimed. "We would never have found Corey without you!"

As she spoke a ray of moonlight broke through

the thick treetops. It cast a golden glow on the three ghosts.

"I-I guess I believe you," I stammered.

"We're telling the truth," Kate replied. "Really."

"I-I guess this could be kind of cool," I stuttered. "You'll be able to tell me everything I ever wanted to know about ghosts. I can come out to the tree house every day and you can—"

"Sorry, Dylan," Corey interrupted me. "We've been stuck on earth a long time. You brought us together. Now we can leave."

And with that, the beam of moonlight began to shimmer. Steve and I watched in awe as it expanded to form a wide, sparkling bridge. It stretched from the moon all the way down to the clearing. It was the most beautiful thing I had ever seen.

The three ghosts reached out and touched Steve and me one last time. Their fingers felt soft and fluttery, like a gentle breeze. As we looked at them, they started to fade and become even more transparent.

Then they joined hands and stepped onto the bridge of light. Kate glanced back and waved.

They walked on the shimmering moonbeam.

Up toward the sky.

And then they disappeared.

"Can you believe that?" I asked Steve. "Can you believe that!"

Steve still couldn't speak. But he did manage to nod "yes."

"Well, well, well, Steve, my lad. You finally believe in ghosts!"

21

I felt dazed after the ghosts disappeared. I turned and followed Steve home. With our three friends gone, I also felt strange. Kind of alone.

I walked close to Steve. The woods seemed darker than ever.

Twigs crackled loudly under our shoes. I heard animal moans and strange cries.

Steve stopped. He spun around. "Hey—where are we?"

Nothing looked familiar. "I-I think we went the wrong way," I stammered. I searched for the moon, but trees blocked the light.

"Those ghosts got me all mixed up," Steve

confessed. He turned and pointed. "I think the path is over there."

I followed him, but I couldn't see any path.

Then, in a small, round clearing, I saw a strange sight. Silvery moonlight spilled into the clearing. And in the moonlight, I saw an old swing set. An old-fashioned wooden swing and slide. Worn and rickety-looking.

And on top of the swing set sat a boy. He had long blond curls that shone in the moonlight. He was dressed in a sailor suit, the kind you see kids wearing in very old pictures.

He was so pale. The moonlight seemed to pour right through him.

Was he stuck up there on that battered swing set?

"Help me," he called when Steve and I stepped into the clearing, into the spotlight of silvery moonlight. "Please—help me!"

Steve and I both rolled our eyes and shook our heads. "Here we go again!" I moaned.

GET READY FOR ANOTHER SPOOKY TALE
FROM FEAR STREET:

R. L. STINE'S

GHOSTS OF
FEAR STREET ®

EYE OF THE
FORTUNETELLER

EYE OF THE FORTUNETELLER

Kelsey Moore tried to scream, but the scream stuck in her throat. The giant Sea Serpent whipped her from side to side. It moved so fast that she could barely hold on. And then the green monster began to dive.

Kelsey tightened her grip. The Sea Serpent plunged down. Down. Down.

Kelsey screamed.

She screamed as the Sea Serpent, the biggest, wildest roller coaster at the beach, rounded the last corner and suddenly jerked to a stop.

"Wow!" Drew gasped. "I'm glad that's over."

"What a gyp," Kelsey said as she and Drew climbed

out of their seats. "I can't believe we stood in line for twenty minutes for that. It wasn't scary at all."

"A gyp!" Drew cried. "Are you crazy? It was totally scary."

"No, it wasn't," Kelsey said as they headed for the exit. "Did you ever ride the Exterminator at Echo Ridge? *That's* a scary ride."

"If it wasn't scary, how come you were screaming?" Drew asked.

"Me? Screaming?" Kelsey laughed. *"You* were the one who was screaming."

"I was not," Drew lied.

"Were, too," Kelsey replied. "The same way you screamed on the merry-go-round."

"Very funny," Drew shot back. "I screamed on the merry-go-round when we were six years old."

"Yeah, I know," Kelsey said. "It scared you so much, you haven't been on it since."

Drew reached out and yanked Kelsey's ponytail.

"Cut it out!" she yelled. But she wasn't really angry. Kelsey and Drew were best friends—and cousins. Cousins who looked practically liked twins.

They both had the same curly blond hair, the same freckles, the same green eyes. They even had the same last name. And they were the same age, too. Twelve. But Kelsey liked to brag that she was older—even if it was only by three weeks.

Every year their parents rented a house together at

the beach. And every year Kelsey had to drag Drew on all the rides. She loved them. He hated them.

It had taken Kelsey two whole summers to convince Drew to ride the Sea Serpent. And after all that, it was a total letdown.

"I'm telling you," Kelsey said. "I've had scarier walks to school."

"I know. I know. You live on Fear Street. There are ghosts and monsters there every day," Drew replied.

"The stories about Fear Street are true," Kelsey insisted. "Really strange things happen to people who live there."

"Nothing weird has happened to you," Drew pointed out.

"Not yet," Kelsey said. But she had plenty of stories to tell about the ghosts that haunted her neighborhood. And she told them to Drew about twice a day.

Drew rolled his eyes. "Okay. You're from Fear Street. Nothing scares you. Nothing except sand crabs."

"They don't scare me," Kelsey lied. "I just think they're gross, that's all. So what do you want to do now?" she asked, changing the subject.

"Go on the bumper cars?" Drew suggested.

"We can't," Kelsey replied. "We don't have enough money left."

3

"What are you talking about?" Drew started digging through his pockets. "We had almost ten dollars each."

"Drew, we've been on about a hundred rides," Kelsey began. And we spent a fortune trying to win that stupid prize you wanted."

"It's not stupid," Drew insisted. "That video game costs eighty bucks in the store. We could win it down here for only a quarter."

"If we could win it for a quarter, how come we've already spent *fifty* of them trying to get it? Besides, there's no way to win anything on those giant wheel games. They're rigged."

"That's not what you said last year," Drew reminded her. "Remember when you made us spend all our money trying to win that pink baby elephant?"

"Oh, yeah," Kelsey replied. "I remember—we didn't win one single game."

"Well, this time it's going to be different. This time we're going to win that video game," Drew declared.

"Okay, okay," Kelsey gave in. "But we should head home now. It's almost time for dinner. We'll try to win it tomorrow—when we can get more money."

Kelsey and Drew headed toward the part of the boardwalk that led to the exit.

4

"I have a little change left," Drew said, still searching through his pockets. "Let's buy some saltwater taffy—" Drew turned to Kelsey, but she was gone.

"Kelsey?"

"Over here," she called from around a corner. "Check this out."

"What is it?" Drew asked, turning the bend.

Kelsey stood in front of a creepy old shack. It was made of wood. Splintered, rotted wood that smelled ancient and moldy.

The small building sagged—the right side stood higher than the left. Kelsey tried to peer through one of the grimy windows, but it was covered with thick iron bars. Heavy black curtains draped the panes.

"I don't know what this is," Kelsey said, circling the strange old shack. "I've never seen it before."

Kelsey glanced up and spotted a sign that hung over the doorway. *"The Amazing Zandra,"* she read, trying to sound spooky. "It's a stupid gypsy fortune-telling place—only the Amazing Zandra is 'Out to Lunch.'" Kelsey pointed to the sign.

Drew pressed his nose up against the window in the door to peek inside. He leaped back, crashing into Kelsey.

"Ouch!" she cried out, rubbing her foot. "What's the matter with you?"

5

"Take a look," Drew whispered.

Kelsey pressed her nose up against the dirty window. She peered into the dark room. Squinting.

Then she saw it.

A skeleton.

A human skeleton. It stared at her with its hollow eyes.

She inhaled sharply. Then laughed.

"It's just a skeleton. A prop," she told Drew. "Fortunetellers use stuff like that all the time. To make you think they're spooky and mysterious."

Kelsey jiggled the doorknob. The door opened with a loud click. "Let's go in!"

"No way," Drew told her, stepping back from the door. "We don't have time. We'll be late for dinner."

"You're such a chicken," Kelsey taunted.

"I am not," Drew shot back. "There's just no reason to go in. Fortunetellers are fakes. Everyone knows that. They can't really tell the future."

Kelsey pulled the door open wide enough to stick her head inside. The air inside the shack felt icy cold. It sent a chill down her spine.

She glanced around the room. A layer of thick dust carpeted the floor. Old books were scattered everywhere.

Kelsey's gaze shifted to the far wall of the shack,

where bookshelves rose from the floor to the ceiling. On them sat tons and tons of stuffed animals.

Kelsey stared at the animals. They weren't like the ones she had in her room.

These were real animals.

Real dead animals.

"You're not going to believe what's in here," Kelsey whispered. "Let's go in."

"No way!" Drew repeated. Then he tugged Kelsey back. "Let's go. We'll be here all summer. We can come back another time."

Kelsey sighed. "Oh, all right, but—"

"Stay. Stay," a raspy voice called from the back of the shack.

Kelsey and Drew turned in time to see a very old woman make her way to the front of the shack. She pointed a wrinkled, gnarled finger at them. "Come," she said. "Come in."

Kelsey stared at the woman. She wore a red flowered dress that hung down to the floor. Her face was lined with wrinkles. And her mouth twisted in a half sneer. But it was her earrings that Kelsey gaped at.

Dozens of gold rings dangled from each ear. Heavy gold earrings that pulled on her lobes and made them hang low.

She fixed her dark eyes on Kelsey as she spoke again.

Kelsey gasped. The woman had one blue eye and one eye the color of coal.

"Come," the woman beckoned. "Come inside. There is much to tell. Come, Kelsey and Drew."

All the color drained from Drew's face. "Kelsey, how does she know our names?" he murmured. "How does she know?"

2

"**S**he probably heard us talking," Kelsey whispered to Drew.

"But we just walked around the shack. She wasn't there," he replied.

"Maybe she heard us through the windows or something," Kelsey answered. "Trust me, these fortunetellers are all fakes. You said so yourself."

"Come, children," the gypsy woman continued, opening the door wider. "Come inside." Then she gazed over her shoulder. "I have something for you."

"Um, thanks. But we can't," Drew said. "We really have to get home."

The gypsy ignored him. And so did Kelsey. She

9

followed the old woman inside. Drew lunged for Kelsey's arm and tried to pull her back, but Kelsey jerked free.

"You have some pretty neat things in here," Kelsey said to the woman as she stepped inside.

"These are not my things," she replied. Then she sat down behind a round table. "Sit." She motioned to two chairs. "You may call me Madame Valda."

"I thought she was supposed to be the Amazing Zandra," Drew whispered as the two took their seats at the table.

Kelsey shrugged as she watched the gypsy set a folded velvet cloth on the table in front of her. It was bloodred and held something inside it.

"Madame Valda will tell your fortune now," the gypsy announced. Then she opened the cloth to reveal a deck of cards.

"But we don't have any money to pay you, uh, Madame Gypsy," Drew said, standing.

"Madame Valda," the old woman corrected sharply. "I will do it for nothing," her voice softened. "Sit! It is a great honor to have Madame Valda tell your fortune."

"Sit!" Kelsey echoed.

Drew sat. Madame Valda spread the deck of cards out on the table. She began to sing softly in a language Kelsey had never heard.

Kelsey watched as the fortuneteller swirled her head around in a circle. She'd seen fortunetellers in the movies do this. They closed their eyes and sang themselves into some kind of trance.

Only Madame Valda wasn't closing her eyes.

She stared straight ahead. Straight at Kelsey.

This is really creepy, Kelsey thought. A nervous giggle escaped her lips.

Madame Valda didn't seem to notice—or she didn't care.

She continued to sing.

She continued to stare.

Directly into Kelsey's eyes.

Kelsey stared back. She felt as if she were in some kind of trance, too. She couldn't stop gazing into the woman's weird eyes.

Finally Madame Valda's chant came to an end, and she shifted her gaze to the deck of cards on the table.

Kelsey let out a long sigh. She didn't realize she'd been holding her breath.

Madame Valda flipped over three cards. They all had strange symbols on them. Symbols that Kelsey had never seen before.

The gypsy studied the cards for a moment, then turned to Drew.

"Drew Moore," she said. "I see that you are sometimes more a follower than a leader. You must be careful to guard against that. It will get you into trouble. Especially when you let Kelsey make all the decisions."

Kelsey shot a quick glance at Drew. His jaw dropped and his eyes grew wide.

Kelsey squirmed in her chair. *How did she know Drew's last name?* she wondered. *How?* Kelsey knew she never said it. And neither did Drew. Not outside. And not inside.

Then she spotted it. Drew's beach pass. Pinned to his shirt. With his name printed in big red letters, Drew T. Moore. Kelsey laughed out loud as she stared down at her own badge. Then she pointed it out to Drew.

"What is funny?" The old woman snarled.

"Um. Nothing," Kelsey replied.

"Then why do you laugh?" the old woman pressed.

"Well, it's just that your fortunetelling powers aren't all that, um, mysterious," Kelsey confessed.

Drew kicked Kelsey under the table.

"Do you think Madame Valda is a fake?" The old woman's voice rose to a screech.

"I *know* Madame Valda is a fake," Kelsey replied, imitating the gypsy's accent.

"You have insulted the famous Madame Valda," the fortuneteller roared. She jerked to her feet and loomed over Kelsey. "Apologize now, or live the rest of your life in fear."

"In fear of what?" Kelsey asked, staring directly into Madame Valda's dark eye. "I'm not afraid of you."

"Oh, yes, you are!" Madame Valda cried. "I am the most powerful fortuneteller who ever lived. And I know all your fears, you foolish child. All your fears!"

"Just say you're sorry and let's go," Drew said, pushing his chair from the table. Then he added in a whisper, "She's worse than scary—she's nuts."

"No," Kelsey told Drew. "I am *not* afraid."

Madame Valda's eyes flickered. She leaned in, closer to Kelsey. Kelsey could feel the gypsy's hot breath on her face. Then she whispered, "Only a fool is not afraid."

Before Kelsey could reply, the old woman reached down and flipped over the next card in the deck. She threw it down onto the table in front of Kelsey.

It looked like a joker.

Kelsey read the words on the bottom of the card—the Fool.

"The cards never lie! You are the fool, and I curse you for the rest of your life. Now get out!" she cried. "Get out. Now!"

Kelsey and Drew jumped up and bolted for the door. Madame Valda's voice thundered behind them. "You will believe. You will know *fear.*"

As soon as Kelsey's and Drew's feet hit the boardwalk, they broke into a run.

But Madame Valda's voice trailed after them. "Fear! Fear! Fear!" she cried out over their pounding sneakers. "You will know fear!"

Kelsey and Drew ran faster. But Madame Valda's voice seemed as close as before. Kelsey glanced back. "Oh, no!" she cried. "She is crazy! She's coming after us!"

3

Kelsey's heart pounded as she ran faster.

Her lungs felt as if they were about to explode.

She turned back—and there was Madame Valda. Right behind her!

This is unreal, Kelsey's mind whirled. How could an old lady run so fast?

"She's right behind us!" Drew cried out, panting.

"Leave us alone!" Kelsey screamed over her shoulder.

Madame Valda's right eye burned into Kelsey— and Kelsey stopped running.

"Run! Run!" Drew screamed.

But Kelsey couldn't move. She felt paralyzed. Frozen in place by the dark eye of the fortuneteller.

The gypsy reached out and clutched Kelsey's shoulder with her bony fingers. A sharp pain shot down Kelsey's arm. She tried to jerk away, but Madame Valda held her tightly.

The old gypsy laughed. A hideous laugh.

"Not afraid!" she cackled. "Oh, yes. You will be afraid!" She whisked the Fool card before Kelsey's eyes, then tossed it in the air.

"Fool! Fool! Fool!" she cried. "Only a fool is not afraid!"

Kelsey and Drew watched as the card flew up. And up. And up. Until it faded to a white flicker in the sky. Then it was gone.

Kelsey wrenched free of Madame Valda's grip, and she and Drew flew down the boardwalk. She ran so fast, her lungs burned in her chest. She quickly glanced back—to see if the fortuneteller was still following them.

But Madame Valda was gone.

"Drew! Stop!" Kelsey grabbed her cousin's arm. "Look! Madame Valda. She disappeared."

Drew spun around. Kelsey was right. Madame Valda had simply vanished.

"How did she run so fast?" Drew asked, out of breath.

"I don't know," Kelsey replied, shaking her head. "Do you think she really was a fortuneteller? I mean, a *real* fortuneteller? With *real* powers?"

"Come on, Kelsey," Drew replied. "Now you sound as crazy as that old hag."

"Yeah, you're right," Kelsey said. But she didn't sound as if she meant it. "So, um, you don't think she put a curse on us, right?" Kelsey asked.

"Not on me," Drew answered. "I was nice to her, remember?"

"Thanks a lot." Kelsey punched Drew in the arm.

"Come on, Kelsey," Drew said. "She probably isn't even a real gypsy."

Kelsey knew that Drew was probably right. But she kept picturing the fortuneteller's strange eyes. And she kept hearing her voice. That horrible voice screaming, "Fool! Fool! Fool!"

"Forget the fortuneteller." Drew headed toward the exit. "We've got real problems. We're late for dinner."

Kelsey checked her watch. "Oh, no!" she groaned. "We're already a half hour late. Mom's going to kill us!"

Kelsey and Drew hurried out the exit. They were only eight blocks from the beach house. If they ran, they'd be home in five minutes.

"Let's take the shortcut home," Kelsey suggested as she dashed ahead of Drew. "It's right there." She pointed ahead. "The alley that runs behind the Italian restaurant."

Drew followed Kelsey past the restaurant and into the narrow, winding alley.

"Where does this go?" Drew asked as they sprinted around the alley's turns and curves.

"To the parking lot on Eighteenth Street," Kelsey answered. "Then we'll be only two blocks from home."

But as they rounded the last curve, Kelsey knew something was wrong. She faced a dead end—a sooty brick wall that rose at least twenty feet high. No parking lot.

"This is really strange," she said, glancing around the alley. It was dark and dingy. Totally deserted. "I'm sure there was a parking lot here last summer."

"Maybe they bricked it up during the winter," Drew suggested. "Let's just get out of here."

Kelsey started back the way they came. Drew followed. But when they reached the other end of the alley—nothing looked the same! Even the Italian restaurant was gone.

Kelsey eyes darted left and right.

"Hey! What's going on?" she cried. "This is so weird. Where are we?"

"I don't know," Drew answered, searching for a street sign. "This has to be the way we came in."

"The restaurant was right on this corner," Kelsey said. "I know it was."

Kelsey stared at the spot where the restaurant should have been. In its place stood an old shingled house with boarded-up windows.

"I don't get it," she mumbled to herself. She'd been coming to this town practically forever. She knew every square inch of it. But suddenly she had no idea where she was.

She glanced around. The alley now led into a street. When Kelsey looked down the street, she noticed a few rundown shacks. Nothing more. In the other direction the street was dark and gloomy and lined with battered houses and abandoned storefronts.

"All right," Kelsey said, trying to stay calm. "The beach must be that way." She pointed to her right. "So that means our house must be this way." Kelsey motioned to the gloomy street.

"That way?" Drew gasped. "I've never even seen that street before. It's totally creepy. We're not going down there."

"I'm telling you, that's the way we have to go," Kelsey insisted and began jogging down the dreary block. "Come on!"

Drew followed her for about three blocks—until she stopped.

"Wait," Kelsey said, out of breath. "This can't be right."

"I told you this wasn't the way to go," Drew muttered. "There aren't any creepy old buildings like these anywhere near our house."

"I know. I know," Kelsey replied. "We'd better ask somebody for directions."

"Like who?" Drew asked.

Good question, Kelsey realized. She gazed up and down the street. There was no one to ask. She and Drew were all alone.

"Where is everybody anyway?" Drew asked. "There should be tons of people everywhere—we're right by the beach."

"The beach," Kelsey repeated. "That's it. We should head for the beach. Then we'll be able to find our way home."

Before Drew could reply, Kelsey took off down a side street. A street she was certain headed toward the shore. But when she reached the next corner, her heart sank.

Nothing but shabby houses. Gutted storefronts. Every way she turned.

No people. No beach.

Kelsey was beginning to think that she and Drew would be lost forever. Tiny beads of sweat formed on her forehead. She wiped them away with the back of her hand.

"This is getting really scary," Drew said when he caught up to her. He glanced down and kicked a jagged piece of glass on the sidewalk.

"What was that?" Kelsey jumped back.

"Just a broken piece of glass," Drew answered.

"No. That—listen," Kelsey replied.

A dog.

Kelsey caught sight of it first.

A big, mangy yellow dog.

She gasped. It was the biggest dog she had ever seen. And it was headed straight for them.

"Let's get out of here!" she screamed.

They crossed the street and charged ahead, but the dog ran faster. Gaining on them. Its wild barks echoed in Kelsey's ears.

Kelsey and Drew stopped on the next corner to catch their breath. They ducked into a darkened doorway, pressing their backs against the door's iron gate. Gasping for air.

They listened.

Silence.

"Do you think it's gone?" Drew asked.

"I-I don't know," Kelsey stammered. "I'll check." She poked her head out from their hiding place.

A pair of crazed yellowed eyes met hers.

The dog sat on its haunches—just a few feet away. It growled. A low growl that exposed two decayed fangs—dripping with saliva.

"Run!" Kelsey cried, grabbing Drew's hand.

The two bolted from the doorway. They flew down the street, holding hands, with Kelsey in the lead.

Kelsey glanced behind her. The dog tore after them. Howling now. And snapping its jaws hungrily.

Kelsey turned down a narrow alleyway. It looked just like the first alley. Only darker. Much darker. And the farther they ran, the narrower it grew.

They dodged around splintered pieces of wood. Shards of glass.

The wild beast charged up behind them, snarling. Its wet, gray tongue hung from its mouth. Kelsey could almost feel the animal's sharp teeth sink into her ankles.

"Faster!" she screamed. "Run faster!"

With a burst of speed the two raced ahead, leaving the dog a few yards behind.

The alley curved sharply to the right. Drew nearly stumbled as the two took the turn.

And then Kelsey stopped. What lay ahead of her was suddenly as terrifying as the wild dog behind her.

Another dead end.

There was no way out.

"We're trapped!" Kelsey shrieked. "We're trapped!"

4

Kelsey and Drew pressed their backs against the building. Waiting. Waiting for the vicious dog to appear.

Kelsey held her breath and listened.

No barking. No snarling.

"Maybe we lost him," she whispered.

"I don't think so," Drew whispered back.

Kelsey silently agreed. The alley went only one way. That dog would have to be pretty stupid to lose track of us, she thought.

"But why isn't he attacking?" she asked Drew.

"I don't know," he replied, shaking his head.

The two waited in silence. The blood pounded in Kelsey's head.

Another minute passed—the longest minute in Kelsey's life—with no sign of the dog. "We can't just stand here, Drew," Kelsey said, finally breaking the quiet. "I'm going to check."

Kelsey tiptoed to the curve in the alley. She peeked around the corner. Slowly.

The alley stood deserted.

No dog.

"It's gone!" Kelsey gasped.

"This is so weird," Drew replied, making his way to her side. "How could it just disappear like that?"

"I don't know. And I don't care. Let's get out of here. Now," Kelsey answered. "Um, you go first."

"Gee, thanks a lot," Drew said as he started down the alley.

They walked quickly but carefully.

Listening.

Listening for any sign of the deadly beast. But the only sound they heard was the soft thumping of their own feet.

The alley seemed even darker than before. And for the first time Kelsey noticed how sour it smelled. The stench flooded her nostrils and made her sick.

"Look!" Drew exclaimed. He stopped short, and Kelsey slammed into him.

"What?" she asked. Her heart skipped a beat. She was afraid to hear the answer.

"I can't believe it!" Drew shouted. "Look where we are!"

Kelsey inched alongside Drew and peered out of the dark alleyway—into bright sunlight.

She knew immediately where she was. But she glanced up at the street sign for proof.

Thirteenth Street.

Less than a block away from their house.

"I thought we were totally lost," Drew said as he started toward their street. He let out a long sigh. "And all the time we were less than a block away from home. That's the last time I follow *you*," he added.

Kelsey was about to shoot back a smart remark of her own when she remembered something strange. Really strange.

"Drew, do you remember what the fortuneteller told you? You know, about getting into trouble if you follow me all the time? You don't think . . ."

A shiver of fear crept down Kelsey's spine. She stopped to glance back at the alleyway.

But it was gone!

You will believe. You will know fear. The fortuneteller's words echoed in Kelsey's mind.

I'm going crazy, Kelsey thought. The alley is there. It must be there. I probably can't see it from this angle—that's all.

"Come on, Kelsey," Drew called. "We're really late!"

25

Kelsey broke into a run. The two raced the rest of the way home. As they neared their house, they spotted their parents sitting outside on the front porch.

"Where have you been?" Kelsey's mother asked.

"Do you know how late it is?" Drew's mother added.

"Sorry," Kelsey apologized. "We got . . ." She was about to say lost, but she stopped herself. If she told them they were lost, she knew what would happen. Their parents would never allow them to go out by themselves anymore. "We were having so much fun on the boardwalk, we lost track of the time."

"We won't do it again," Drew added. "We promise."

"All right." Her mother forgave her more quickly than she ever did at home.

That was one of the best things about being on vacation. Parents were so much easier to get along with.

"Come inside and wash your hands for dinner," Drew's mother instructed. Then their parents led the way inside.

As Kelsey climbed the porch steps, she thought about the old fortuneteller again. Now that she was safe at home, the whole thing seemed pretty dumb.

"Fool!" Kelsey heard the echo of the old gypsy woman's voice. Only this time she started to laugh at herself—for acting like one.

Kelsey was about to step through the front door when something caught her eye. Something falling from the sky. Fluttering. Fluttering. Down. Down. Down.

Drew spotted it, too. "What is that?" he asked, squinting as he gazed up.

"I can't tell," Kelsey replied, watching the object float down on a breeze.

And then it landed right at Kelsey's feet.

She gasped.

It was the card.

The card that the old gypsy woman had tossed into the air.

Kelsey trembled as she stared at it. As she stared down into the face of the Fool.

5

That night Kelsey sat on her bed, alone in her room, staring at the Fool card.

"*You* are the Fool, Madame Whatever-your-name-is," Kelsey muttered. "And you are *not* going to scare me. No way."

Kelsey turned the card over and over in her hand. Then she ripped it in half. Then ripped it in half again. And again. "So there!" she declared when she was through.

She scooped up every last bit of paper and dumped it all into the wastepaper basket near her dresser.

"Tomorrow will be a much better day," she promised herself as she slipped between the sheets. Then she closed her eyes.

She pictured herself at the beach with Drew. They would spend the whole day there, she decided. Swimming in the ocean. Collecting shells. Playing volleyball. Lying in the sun.

Kelsey could imagine the warmth of the sun on her skin as she snuggled into her pillow. It felt good—even in her imagination.

Then she started to drift off to sleep—pretending that she was already on the beach.

But something tickled her left foot. She rubbed at it with her right one.

But the tickle returned.

Now it moved up the back of her leg.

Kelsey brushed her leg against the sheet. But it didn't work. The tickle kept moving—moving up her leg.

Only now it wasn't a tickle. It felt prickly.

Kelsey brushed her leg with her foot. But the prickly feeling didn't go away.

It started to spread.

Over her legs. Her arms. Her whole body.

She tried to ignore it.

She fluffed her pillow and rolled over on her side. But that didn't work, either.

Now it felt as though her whole bed had come alive. With tiny little legs.

Millions of them.

Skittering across her body.

Crawling into her hair. Stinging her skin.

She shot up in bed. She stared at the sheets. At her body. But it was too dark to see.

And then she felt it.

A tiny set of legs creeping across her cheek.

And she knew what it was.

Sand crabs! Even in the dark, she knew. She hated sand crabs—they terrified her!

She shrieked with horror.

Her hands flew to her legs. Her arms. Her face. Frantically trying to brush the creatures away.

"Get off!" she cried. "Get off!"

But within seconds they swarmed over her entire body.

Kelsey grew frightened. So frightened that she couldn't breathe.

She tried to scream. But all that came out was a choked whimper—as she felt one of the disgusting little creatures start to crawl inside her ear.

6

Kelsey leaped out of bed.

She threw her head from side to side. "Get out!" she screamed. "Get out!"

The stinging in her ear stopped. But her hair felt alive. Alive with the horrible creatures.

She scratched her head. Scratched until her scalp turned raw.

She had to look in the mirror. She had to see the crabs. To see where they were. To get them off.

She flipped on the light switch and headed for the mirror over her dresser. She didn't want to look. She didn't want to see those disgusting crabs—with their hideous pincers creeping on her skin.

But she forced herself to look.

And then she screamed.

No sand crabs.

Not in her hair. Not on her face.

Nowhere.

She spun around to face her bed—expecting to see it crawling with sand crabs.

Nothing there, either. Nothing but her clean blue sheets and plump white pillow.

Kelsey quickly pulled back the cover. No creatures hiding anywhere.

What is going on? she wondered. *What is wrong with me?* She glanced over at her clock—2:00 A.M. Suddenly she felt exhausted.

She checked her bed once more before dropping into it. But she couldn't fall asleep. Her skin still felt tingly. Still felt as if thousands of tiny legs were creeping all over it.

She thought about the creatures. She pictured them swarming all over her body. A low groan escaped her lips.

What if they come back? She shuddered.

She propped up her pillows and decided to stay up all night. But she was tired. So tired. And before she knew it, she drifted off to sleep.

The early dawn light fell upon Kelsey's face and woke her up. She turned over her pillow and tried to fall back asleep—but she heard something. Something nearby.

Her eyes popped open and searched the room.

There it was.

On the floor.

A sand crab. A single sand crab.

Kelsey watched in horror as it skittered across her floor and darted under her bed.

Oh, no! She gasped. What if there were millions of sand crabs. Millions of them under her bed. Waiting for her.

Her heart pounded in her chest. Her temples throbbed. But she knew she had to look. She had to know.

Kelsey checked the floor carefully before she slid out of bed. Then she kneeled down and peered underneath the bed, into the darkness.

She spotted her slippers. An old *Teen* magazine. And a lot of dust.

Then she saw it.

Not the sand crab. Not even a thousand sand crabs.

It was something much more horrible.

Kelsey's lower lip trembled. Her hands began to shake.

She squeezed her eyes shut, hoping that when she opened them, the terrible thing would be gone. Just the way all those sand crabs had disappeared.

But when she opened her eyes, it was still there.

33

The Fool card that she had ripped to shreds.

There it was.

Under her bed.

All in one piece.

A ray of sunlight filtered through her window and fell upon the card. And Kelsey could see the Fool's menacing grin—the menacing grin that was meant just for her.

7

"**S**o were the crabs real or not?" Drew asked.

Kelsey told Drew all about her terrible night as the two walked to the beach the next morning.

"I told you!" Kelsey yelled. "They weren't real. Well, one of them was real. But not the others."

"So—why were you afraid?"

"Look!" Kelsey said, shoving the Fool card right in his face.

"So?" Drew pushed her hand away.

"So!" Kelsey couldn't believe that he could be so dumb. "I told you. I tore it up into a million pieces and threw it into the garbage can! Now look at this thing. It isn't even bent or creased."

"This just doesn't make any sense," Drew said as

they reached the beach and started tromping through the sand.

"Wow, Drew. When did you become such a genius?"

"Very funny," Drew grumbled. "So—what are you going to do?"

"Well, I am definitely not going to let that old gypsy and her stupid curse scare me," Kelsey declared. "And now I am going to get rid of this card—forever."

Kelsey headed directly to the ocean. She stood on the shore for a few moments and watched the waves roll in.

"What are you doing?" Drew asked.

"Watch," she told him. She held up the Fool card and tore it again and again and again—until she couldn't tear it anymore.

Then, with Drew by her side, she waded out into the water. When the first wave broke around her knees, she scattered some of the bits of paper over the water.

She and Drew watched as the foam carried them away.

When the next wave hit, she did the same thing, scattering a little more of what was left of the card. Wave after wave, she did the same thing—until nothing was left.

"There," she said as the surf carried off the last torn pieces. "It's gone for good. Now let's go swimming."

"We have to wait for our parents," Drew reminded her. "You know the rules. 'No swimming, kids, unless we're with you.'"

"Yeah, yeah, I know. But they promised they were coming out right away," Kelsey complained. "Where are they anyway?"

She scanned the beach, searching for them. "There they are!" she said, spotting them.

Kelsey jumped up and down, waving at their parents to get their attention. When they waved back, Kelsey darted into the ocean.

"Race you to France," she called over her shoulder to Drew.

Drew dived in after her.

They fought their way through crashing waves until they were shoulder-deep in the water. Kelsey watched as a wave began to swell behind them.

"Let's ride this one," she yelled.

"All right!" Drew yelled back.

Kelsey bent her knees and pushed off the sandy floor. Drew did the same. The wave took them on an awesome ride. Perfect all the way to the end.

They swam out and waited to catch the next wave. Suddenly Kelsey felt something squishy hit her back. And it stayed there—right between her shoulders.

"Drew," she called. "Do you see something on my back?"

But Drew wasn't there. He had caught the wave and was headed for the shore.

She reached over her shoulder to swat off whatever was there. The tips of her fingers brushed against something soft.

Something wet and slimy.

Something that began to wriggle against her skin.

"Jellyfish!" she shrieked in terror.

She tried to brush it off, but it wouldn't budge.

She jumped up and down and tried to shake it off. The more she struggled with it, the tighter it clung to her.

Digging into her back.

Stinging her with its deadly poison.

8

"**D**rew!" Kelsey screamed. "Drew! Help me!"

But Drew was riding his wave to the shore. He couldn't hear her.

Kelsey dug her nails into her back. Trying to scratch the jellyfish off. Her fingers sunk into its gooey body. And with a sickening *thwop*, it closed around her hand.

"Help me!" she screamed. "Somebody, help me!" She twisted and turned until she wrenched her hand free.

Get back to shore, she thought. *That's what I have to do!*

A wave began to swell. I'll ride it in, Kelsey decided. It will be the fastest way back.

As soon as it reached her, Kelsey pushed off and tried to catch it. But her timing was off, and she missed. She tried for the next one. But the wave seemed to wash right over her.

She missed wave after wave. And it seemed like the harder she tried, the faster the waves passed her by.

Her skin started to burn under the creature's slimy hold.

"Swim in!" she told herself. "Just get to shore and get help!"

Kelsey paddled as hard as she could. But she seemed to be moving in slow motion. She noticed that the water around her was churning. Growing thick and cloudy.

She swam harder. Her hands thrashed the water. But she felt as if she were swimming in Jell-O.

Why is it so hard to move? she wondered. Why am I stuck in the same spot?

The jellyfish on her back gripped her skin. A sharp pain shot through her body.

Kelsey kicked her legs. Harder and harder.

Her arms ached. And the muscles in her shins were beginning to cramp. With every move, she gasped for breath. But she had to get to shore. She had to get that jellyfish off her back.

I must be close to the beach now, Kelsey thought.

She looked up.

She was farther away than when she started!

"How can that be?" she screamed.

She needed to rest before she tried to make her way back again. She closed her eyes. Then she flipped over on her back and floated for a few seconds—until she felt something on her shoulders.

She turned her head from side to side.

Two blobs rested on her shoulders.

Two hideous bluish blobs.

Jellyfish!

Giant blue blobs of jellyfish!

The shiny blue blob that sucked on her right shoulder was chunky and clear. But the one on her left shoulder had little red lines running through it.

Poisonous! She was certain.

She flipped over quickly, but before she could peel the horrible creatures off, her legs began to sting. Then her arms. Then her stomach and the back of her neck. Even the soles of her feet.

"They're all over me!" she shrieked.

Some were small—like clear jellybeans. Others had tentacles that shimmered in the water. They curled around her limbs. Closing around them. Tighter and tighter.

A tiny one was stuck to Kelsey's eyelash. Every time she blinked, she looked through its slimy, cloudy body.

41

Kelsey's heart raced. She felt dizzy. Everything around her started to spin.

Don't panic! she told herself. *Swim!*

Kelsey's arms sliced through the water as she struggled toward the shore.

But swimming grew harder and harder.

The water felt thick and gooey.

She was swimming in a sea of jellyfish!

Kelsey's eyes darted around her. There were jellyfish everywhere. There seemed to be more jellyfish than water. Waves of jellyfish rolled toward her. Crashing against her skin with a sickening splat.

She flailed through the sea of slime. "I'm not going to make it," she groaned. "I'm not going to make it back."

The jellyfish sea thickened around her. She could barely lift her arms to swim anymore.

And then a huge wave lifted her up and carried her toward the shore. As soon as her foot hit the ocean's sandy bottom, she stood up and charged out of the water.

"Help me!" she screamed. "Somebody, help me get these things off!"

But the people on the beach didn't move.

Why wasn't anyone helping her? What was wrong with them?

"Kelsey!" Drew shouted. She spun around to face him. "What is wrong with you?"

"Jellyfish! Jellyfish!" was all Kelsey could say, shaking her stinging arms and legs.

"What jellyfish?" Drew asked, staring out into the ocean.

"The ones all over me!" Kelsey cried. "Look!"

"Kelsey," Drew replied, "there are no jellyfish on you."

9

Kelsey stared at her arms. She stretched out her legs and searched them. She ran her fingers through her hair.

No jellyfish.

"There *were* jellyfish," Kelsey insisted, rubbing the skin on her arms, trying to get rid of the slimy feeling she still had. "They were all over me! And the whole ocean was full of them!"

Kelsey noticed that the people all around them were listening to her—trying not to laugh.

"Do you see them now?" Drew asked.

Kelsey stared into the water. She and Drew stood there.

Silently.

Watching the water wash up around their feet.

Clean, clear water. Not a jellyfish in sight.

"No," Kelsey admitted. "But something really creepy is going on."

"I'll say," Drew agreed.

"You don't think I'm going nuts, do you?" she asked.

"Nah," he answered. "You're not *going* nuts. You *are* nuts."

"Ha, ha." Kelsey tried to smile.

Then she felt something hit her ankle. And she jumped away, practically knocking Drew over.

"Jellyfish!" she screamed before she could stop herself.

Drew looked down.

Kelsey saw his face freeze in horror.

"Is it a jellyfish?" she cried. "Is it?"

"No," Drew whispered. "Not a jellyfish."

Kelsey slowly glanced down. There, lying at her feet was the Fool card.

All in one piece.

Grinning up at her with its evil grin.

"M-maybe this is a different card," Drew stuttered.

Kelsey kneeled to pick it up. "Drew, I think that fortuneteller really did put a curse on me." She sighed. "I can't believe it. I spend my whole life living on Fear Street and nothing terrible happens to me.

45

But I come down to the shore for a week and I end up with a curse!"

"Look," Drew said nervously, "if you really have been cursed, there's got to be a way to get rid of it, right?"

"How am I supposed to know?" she shot back. "Do I look like a gypsy to you?"

"Well, maybe we should go find that weird old lady again," he started. "And maybe if you apologize to her, she'll take the curse off."

"She should apologize to me," Kelsey said. "She's ruining my vacation."

"Get real, Kelsey. We've got to do something."

"Okay, okay." Kelsey agreed. "Let's go find that stupid witch."

Kelsey told their parents that she and Drew were going to play some skeet ball at the arcade. Then they headed for the boardwalk to search for the old gypsy woman.

"What am I supposed to say when we find her?" Kelsey asked Drew. "I'm sorry I thought you were a fake—please take this curse off of me?"

"That sounds pretty good," Drew said as they headed down the boardwalk. "Look. Here's the pizza place. The shack should be right around this corner."

Kelsey followed Drew around the corner—and there it was. As Kelsey approached it, a horrible thought crossed her mind.

What if the gypsy refuses to remove the curse?
What would she do then?

"Are you ready?" Drew asked, walking up to the door.

Kelsey nodded.

Drew opened the door and Kelsey stepped inside.

The skeleton was still there. But now it seemed to be staring right at her. Following her every move.

Kelsey shivered.

Then from a darkened corner a voice called out, "Welcome." Kelsey stared at the figure. She sat at the table, staring into her crystal ball.

But something about her wasn't right.

"Welcome," the shadowed figure called again. Even though Kelsey couldn't see her face, she knew that it wasn't the same gypsy.

"The Amazing Zandra will tell your fortune," the woman continued, without any kind of accent at all.

When the Amazing Zandra finally glanced up, Kelsey could see that she wasn't nearly as spooky. Or nearly as old as the other gypsy.

In fact, the Amazing Zandra didn't look much older than Kelsey's next-door neighbor—who just started high school last year.

Kelsey even thought she was kind of pretty. Her wavy hair was long and brown. And her eyes were ordinary. Brown. Both of them.

Zandra's fingernails were painted purple. And she

47

had a ring on every finger. She wasn't nearly as mysterious or spooky as Madame Valda.

"I have to see the other gypsy," Kelsey announced.

"There is no other gypsy," Zandra informed them.

"Yes, there is," Drew said. "She was here yesterday. She's really old and wrinkly."

"You must be mistaken," Zandra insisted. "There is no other gypsy here. And there never has been."

Kelsey felt her heart sink.

"Oh, no," she moaned. "Now what am I going to do? I'm going to be cursed forever!"

10

"**A**re you sure there isn't another gypsy?" Drew asked again.

"Look, kid," Zandra replied. "I'm the gypsy who works here, okay? The only gypsy. Now do you want me to tell your fortune or not?"

The Amazing Zandra is lying to us, Kelsey thought. She has to be.

"Look, Amazing Zandra," Kelsey said as politely as she could. "We were here yesterday. But you weren't. There was a different gypsy. She was real, *real* old."

"And scary," Drew added.

But Zandra just kept shaking her head no.

"She had a really strange accent," Kelsey went on.

Nothing. Just more head-shaking from Zandra.

"She put a curse on me," Kelsey said hopelessly.

With that, Zandra's expression changed. "A curse?" she gasped, clutching her heart. "If you are under the curse of a gypsy, you are in very serious trouble."

"Tell me about it," Kelsey said.

"Perhaps I *can* help you," the Amazing Zandra replied.

"Really?" Kelsey asked nervously.

"Yes, really," Zandra answered. "Only it isn't easy to remove a curse," she added. "And it isn't cheap, either."

"How much?" Kelsey asked Zandra.

"Ten dollars."

"Ten dollars!" Kelsey gasped.

That was a lot of money. It was all the money she had. She had planned to spend it on carnival games and rides and ice cream.

But she had no choice. She didn't know if Zandra was a real gypsy or not. But she was her only hope.

She handed the money over to the fortuneteller. "Take the curse off me," she told her.

"First you must explain to me exactly how you were cursed," Zandra said. "Did the old gypsy give the curse a name?"

"No," Kelsey said. "But she called me a name."

"And what was that?" Zandra asked.

"A fool," Kelsey told her. "And she got real mad at me for not believing in her."

Zandra shook her head gravely.

"Now all these terrible things are happening to me," Kelsey continued. "Yesterday, we got lost. And last night hundreds of sand crabs attacked me in my sleep."

"And this morning," Drew jumped in, "she thought she was smothered in jellyfish."

Zandra cringed.

"And no matter what I do," Kelsey went on, "I can't seem to get rid of this card." Kelsey placed the Fool card down on the table in front of Zandra.

"I've torn it up twice. But it just keeps coming back, right after something really bad happens to me."

"Ah," Zandra nodded knowingly. "The Fool Card Curse. This is a very powerful curse," she told Kelsey. "But the Amazing Zandra can remove it."

"Are you sure?" Kelsey asked.

Zandra nodded. Then she closed her eyes and started mumbling, rolling her head around in a circle.

Zandra didn't chant like the old gypsy. And she wasn't using the same weird language, either.

When Zandra finally came out of her trance, she took a thick, red marker and made an X on the face of the Fool card. Then she picked up the card and put it into a metal box—which she snapped shut and locked.

"This card will no longer trouble you," Zandra assured Kelsey.

"Is that it?" Kelsey asked. "Is the curse removed?"

"Not yet," Zandra answered. She reached into another box and pulled out a small object. "You must wear this magic amulet for protection."

It didn't look like a magic amulet to Kelsey. It looked like a crystal bead on a string. But Kelsey took it anyway and slipped it over her head.

"Wear the amulet for three days. Never take it off. And at sundown on the third day, the curse will be broken forever."

Kelsey made it through the rest of the day without any problems at all. And she even made it through the night without any creepy nightmares. So by the next morning she was starting to feel a lot better.

But she wasn't going to take any chances. Not until three days had passed. She and Drew stayed around the house the first day, where it was safe. She actually had a lot of fun playing Ping-Pong and board games. She hardly thought about the curse.

By the second day she felt even braver. Brave enough to go to the arcade.

On the very first quarter she dropped on the Wheel of Fortune, she won the video game Drew wanted!

"Wow! Drew, this charm is great!" she said, fingering the amulet around her neck. "It's working against the curse—and it's bringing me good luck, too!"

By the time she and Drew headed home, they had armfuls of stuffed animals that Kelsey had won.

On the afternoon of the third day, Kelsey was finally brave enough to go to the beach. The sun was shining. The ocean was warm. And Kelsey was feeling pretty confident that Zandra had removed the curse.

Kelsey and Drew started building a very fancy sand castle.

"Let's build a moat around it," she suggested as she dumped another bucket of sand on the castle.

"Good idea," Drew agreed.

"Here," Kelsey said, waving away an annoying horsefly. "Go fill this bucket with water. I'll start digging."

Drew took the bucket and headed for the water.

Kelsey started digging the trench around the castle. She glanced around. Their castle was by far the biggest and fanciest one on the beach. She decided to decorate the top with the beautiful, thin, orangy shells her family always called potato-chip shells.

Bzzz. The pesky horsefly landed on Kelsey's leg.

"Ouch!" Kelsey cried as it bit into her skin. "Go away!" Kelsey shooed the fly away again. She noticed a spot of blood where the horsefly had landed.

Bzzz. The fly circled the castle.

53

Drew came back with his first bucket full of water and poured it into the unfinished trench. The sand sucked it all up.

"We're going to need a lot more than that," Kelsey told him.

"Right," Drew agreed. He headed back to the water, bucket in hand.

Kelsey went back to digging the moat when she felt the tickle of tiny legs on the back of her neck.

The horsefly.

She reached back to shoo it away before it could sting her.

It took off, but it continued to buzz around her as she worked on the castle. She jerked her head from side to side as it swooped down at her.

"Just go!" she yelled at it impatiently.

Finally it landed on a shell near the castle, and she continued her work—until she felt a tickle on her leg. Another horsefly.

Before she could swat at that one, a third appeared, landing right on the tip of her nose.

Kelsey jumped up, flailing her arms to get rid of the horseflies.

"Ouch!" she screamed as she felt a sting on the back of her leg. She looked down to see where she'd been bitten, and noticed that there were three horseflies crawling up her thigh.

"Get off!" she shrieked, trying to swat them away.

But they wouldn't leave. In fact, it seemed that as she fought to get rid of them, more of the horrible green-eyed bugs appeared.

"This can't be happening!" Kelsey cried, reaching up to touch her magic amulet. But the amulet was coated with buzzing horseflies. Horseflies that started stinging her hands the moment she touched the charm.

Kelsey began to feel tiny pinpricks all over her body. Hundreds of horseflies flew at her. Hundreds. Stinging her. Over and over again.

She kicked her legs. Waved her arms.

She ran in circles, trying to dodge the ugly insects. But they followed her. They dived at her.

If she didn't get rid of them, every inch of her body would be bitten and bloody.

Their bulging eyes burned brightly as they buzzed around her head. *Buzz. Buzz. Buzz.*

The black cloud of insects circled her face. Closer and closer.

She couldn't breathe.

"I'm going to choke!" Kelsey screamed. "I'm going to choke!"

She swung her head wildly. Her sweat-drenched body heaved in terror.

The flies still surrounded her. Biting deeper and deeper. Burning her flesh.

She tried to shake off the flies, but there were too many of them now. And she fell to the ground, exhausted.

She gasped for breath. She inhaled deeply. Inhaled a mouthful of sand.

Sputtering, gagging, she headed for the ocean. "I'll drown them! I'll drown them!" she screamed.

She raced to the shore, blinded by the horseflies smothering her face.

"Hey! Watch it!" some little kids yelled as she stumbled over their pails and shovels.

Finally she felt the ocean splash beneath her feet. She was about to dive in. Dive under the cool water to soothe her raw, stinging skin.

But someone grabbed her.

"Let go!" she screamed, squirming to break free.

"Where are you going?" Drew asked, holding fast.

"Into the water," she shrieked. "I have to get these horseflies off me."

Drew didn't reply. He didn't have to. His expression told Kelsey everything she needed to know.

There were no horseflies on her.

Not a single one.

Kelsey collapsed into the sand.

The burning and stinging stopped.

"This stupid amulet didn't work," she uttered hopelessly. "Now what am I going to do?"

"Let's go back to the sand castle. We'll think of something," Drew suggested.

He helped her up, and they headed back to their spot on the beach.

"Oh, no!" Kelsey gasped as their sand castle came into view. She pointed a shaky finger at the top of one of its towers.

Drew followed her gaze. And moaned.

"How could this be?" she wailed.

Sticking out of the very top, fluttering in the breeze, was the Fool card—with a bright red X drawn on its face.

12

"**T**he curse isn't broken!" Kelsey screamed. "It's driving me crazy!" Then she snatched up the card and stomped off.

"Hey! Wait up!" Drew yelled. "Where are you going?"

"Back to the Amazing Zandra," she hollered.

Kelsey broke into a run. Drew chased after her. But she didn't stop until she burst through the door of the Amazing Zandra's shack.

Zandra was sitting behind the table with her feet propped up, flipping through a fashion magazine.

She wore a gypsy dress. But it was hiked up so high that Kelsey could see her cutoff jeans underneath it.

And she didn't have long, dark hair anymore. It was

59

short and blond. The long, dark hair was a wig—and without it, Zandra looked even younger. She didn't look much older than Kelsey.

"You're a fake!" Kelsey shouted at her.

"We've got the card to prove it," Drew added.

Kelsey flung the card down in front of the Amazing Zandra. "Look," she said. "It even has the red X you drew on it. How do you explain that?"

Zandra stared at the card. "Where did you get this?" she asked suspiciously.

"It just appeared," Kelsey told her. "Right after I was attacked by a swarm of horseflies."

"What kind of trick are you two trying to pull on me?" she asked.

"Us?" Kelsey shot back. "You're the one who ripped me off. You said you removed the curse. But you didn't. I was nearly eaten alive by those horseflies! You didn't remove that stupid curse—and this card proves it!"

"That," Zandra declared, "is a different card. The one you brought to me is safely locked inside this box." Then she reached for the metal box and placed it on the table.

"Really?" Kelsey smirked. "Then show it to me."

"No problem," Zandra replied. "I will." She dipped her hand into the pocket of her dress and pulled out the key. She slipped it into the lock and turned it.

60

Zandra hesitated only for a moment before she lifted the lid.

"Oh, no!" She gasped, staring down into the box. "How can this be?"

Kelsey's eyes were glued to the box. She knew exactly what they would find inside.

Nothing.

Zandra tilted it so that Kelsey and Drew could take a look.

But the box wasn't empty.

And Kelsey shrieked when she spotted what was inside.

13

"**O**h, no!" Kelsey cried. "I don't believe this!"

Inside the box was a picture of Kelsey. And there, scrawled across the front, was a big, red *X*. A big red *X* right through Kelsey's face.

The Amazing Zandra studied the Fool card that Kelsey had returned. Then she peered into the box at Kelsey's picture. Then back at the card.

"How did you do this?" Zandra demanded.

"How many times do I have to tell you?" Kelsey shouted. "I didn't do anything. The card keeps coming back all by itself. Because I'm under a curse! That's why I paid you ten dollars in the first place. Remember? To take the curse off!"

"Whoa! This is totally freaky," Zandra said. "It sounds to me like you really *are* under a curse."

"That's what we've been telling you all along!" Drew yelled. "Now, can you do anything to help, or not?"

"I don't know," Zandra shrugged. "I think you probably ought to talk to the gypsy who put the curse on you and ask her to remove it."

"But—but," Kelsey sputtered, "I tried that already. The only time I ever saw her was in here. And you told me that was impossible—that there was no other gypsy!"

"I *am* the only gypsy here," Zandra stated. "What was this other gypsy's name? Did she tell you?"

"Yes," Kelsey answered. "But I don't remember what it was. It was something weird."

"Madame something," Drew reminded her. "Madame . . . Madame . . ."

"Valda!" Kelsey blurted out.

"That's it!" Drew agreed. "Madame Valda!"

Zandra's jaw dropped.

"What's wrong?" Kelsey asked.

"That can't be," Zandra said, shaking her head. "Madame Valda. Here? No," she answered her own question. "That just can't be."

"You know who Madame Valda is?" Drew asked.

"Of course," Zandra answered. "Every gypsy in the world knows who Madame Valda is."

"Well, who is she?" Kelsey asked, planting her hands on her hips.

Zandra took a deep breath. "Madame Valda is the most powerful gypsy who ever lived. And the most evil. But you could not possibly have seen Madame Valda," Zandra assured them.

"Why not?" Kelsey wanted to know.

"Because," Zandra said, staring directly into her eyes, "Madame Valda has been dead for more than a hundred years."

14

"**M**adame Valda can't be dead!" Kelsey shouted. "She was sitting right here! Tell her, Drew!"

"She was," Drew insisted.

"Maybe you're thinking of a different Madame Valda," Kelsey told Zandra.

But Zandra shook her head no. "There is only one Madame Valda," she insisted. "And I'm telling you that she has been dead for a really long time."

"But we saw her!" Drew exclaimed. "So that's impossible!"

"Well," Zandra hesitated for a moment. "Not according to some of the old gypsies, it isn't. But I never believed them."

"What do you mean?" Kelsey asked.

"Well, some of the older gypsies believe that Madame Valda can still appear—even after death."

"Yeah, well, you better believe it now," Kelsey declared. "Because I'm telling you—*she was here!*"

"Oh, man." Zandra cringed. "This is tooooo creepy."

"Tell me about it!" Kelsey shot back. "I'm the one who's been cursed by a dead gypsy!"

"So what do we do now?" Drew asked Zandra.

Zandra shrugged. "You've got me."

"Oh, that's just great!" Kelsey huffed. "Just great!"

"Look, don't panic," Zandra told Kelsey. "I have an uncle. He knows all about the old ways. He's the one who told me about Madame Valda. I bet he can help you."

"Where is he?" Drew asked.

"How soon can we see him?" Kelsey added.

"You can see him right now," Zandra answered as she stood up. "Just wait here. I'll go wake him up."

Kelsey and Drew watched Zandra disappear through a curtain of beads that led into a back room.

Kelsey started to pace nervously.

"Do you believe this!" Kelsey was talking more to herself than to Drew. "A dead gypsy put a curse on me! I hope Zandra's uncle is like Super-gypsy or something. Otherwise, I'm doomed."

"You're not doomed," Drew muttered. He didn't sound very convincing.

Just then the beads parted and Zandra headed toward Kelsey and Drew. An old man followed behind.

The man appeared to be as old as Madame Valda herself. Kelsey thought that was a very good sign.

He wore all black. Black pants, black jacket. A worn black leather vest. On a chain around his neck hung a large blue bead.

When Kelsey peered closer, she realized the bead was really a glass eye!

"This is my uncle, Gregor," Zandra said as she approached them.

"It's nice to meet you, Mr. Gregor," Kelsey said as politely as she could. There was no way in the world she was going to insult another gypsy.

Gregor's wrinkled old face showed no expression. He stood as still as a statue and stared at Kelsey. "Zandra tells me that you think you have been cursed by Madame Valda," he finally said.

Gregor spoke in an accent much like Madame Valda's. And Kelsey thought that was an even better sign.

"I don't *think* I've been cursed," Kelsey told Gregor. "I *know* I've been cursed."

Kelsey told Gregor about the Fool card and Madame Valda. She told him all about getting lost, and about the sand crabs. The jellyfish. The horseflies.

Gregor listened without moving. Without even blinking. When she was finished, he said, "I must tell you, this is most unusual."

"No kidding," Drew blurted out. "Especially since Madame Valda is dead!"

"Death is only a bend in the path for someone as powerful as Madame Valda," Gregor told him.

"A what?" Kelsey's eyes opened wide.

"A bend in the path," Zandra repeated. "It means that death can't stop Madame Valda. It just slows her down for a while."

Kelsey turned to Drew in time to see his jaw drop.

"I told you Madame Valda was the most powerful gypsy who ever lived," Zandra said, as if Kelsey needed to be reminded.

"Yes," Gregor agreed. "She was the most powerful gypsy who ever lived. Only she was evil to the bone. And she used her powers in ways that were unthinkable."

"Like how unthinkable?" Kelsey asked, not really wanting to know.

Gregor just shook his head. He didn't answer Kelsey's question. But he continued with his story.

"Madame Valda was so evil that the other gypsies feared her. They feared her for her power. But they

68

also feared that her evil would cause terrible misfortune for all the other gypsies.

"So, secretly, the other gypsies—her own people—decided to kill her. They selected a young boy and a young girl to sneak into her tent and poison her wine."

"Oh, wow!" Zandra exclaimed. Then she sat down and began fanning herself with her fashion magazine.

Gregor went on.

"How the boy and girl managed to trick her—no one knows. But Valda died. Her dead body was thrown into the sea.

"But Valda did not stay in the sea. She has been seen many times and in many places for over one hundred years. And each time she comes back, it is with evil in her heart."

Neither Kelsey nor Drew could speak after Gregor finished his story. But finally Kelsey managed to break the thick silence. "What happened to the boy and girl who poisoned her?"

"Madame Valda cursed them and eventually they went crazy."

"So do you know how to break Madame Valda's curse?" Zandra asked.

Kelsey held her breath, waiting for the answer.

Gregor nodded yes. "But I must warn you, it will not be easy. It will not be easy at all."

Gregor inched closer to Kelsey. She stared at the blue eye dangling from his neck as he spoke in a deep whisper.

"I can remove the curse," he stated. "But removing it will be terrifying—so terrifying that you may think it is *worse* than the curse itself!"

15

Kelsey shivered. She tried to speak in a normal tone, but her voice came out in a squeak. "I have no choice. I want to break the curse."

"Then you must do exactly as I tell you," Gregor said.

"Fine," Kelsey agreed. "Let's just get this over with."

Gregor's wrinkly old face finally cracked into a smile. In fact, he started to laugh. "But you are not ready yet," he told her.

"I'm as ready as I'll ever be," she insisted.

"No," Gregor said. "You are not. There are many things you must do before we can begin. And we can not begin until midnight."

"How come we can't begin right away?" Kelsey asked.

"You must not ask any questions," Gregor told her. "To remove the curse, I must have your trust."

Trust? I don't trust you at all, Kelsey thought. But she knew there was no point in arguing. "Okay," she said. "No questions."

"Good," Gregor declared. "Now listen to me carefully. The first thing you must do is gather up your fears."

"Ask him what that's supposed to mean," Kelsey whispered to Drew—so she wouldn't break Gregor's rules.

"What exactly does that mean?" Drew asked.

Gregor ignored him. "You will bring me a map," he told Kelsey. "And on it you will circle the street where your beach house is located. Understand?"

Kelsey nodded. At least she really did understand that part, even though she had no idea why Gregor needed a map.

"And you will bring me a sand crab," Gregor continued. "One that is still alive."

"Ewwww, gross," Zandra chimed in.

"Hush, Zandra," Gregor scolded. "You must also bring me a big, buzzing horsefly," he continued. "And a lumpy, fat jellyfish. The boy may assist you in finding these things. But you alone must be the one to catch them."

72

Thinking about touching the crabs and the jellyfish made Kelsey itch all over.

"When you have everything you need, you will come to the gypsy camp. It is under the boardwalk. You must be there by the stroke of midnight," Gregor instructed.

"Don't worry," Kelsey assured him. "We'll be there."

"Good," Gregor said, standing up. "Oh, yes," he added, "there is just one more thing you will need to bring."

"What?" Drew asked.

This time Gregor didn't seem to mind answering Drew's question. "Twenty dollars," he told Drew. "The cost of removing the curse."

And with that, Gregor and Zandra disappeared behind the beads.

Later that afternoon Kelsey started step one of removing the curse: gathering her fears.

The map was easy. She found it in the glove compartment of her mother's car.

Finding a sand crab. That was no problem, either. There were dozens of them crawling around the beach.

But Kelsey couldn't stand to actually touch them. The thought of those creepy, pinchy legs made her skin crawl. So she found a jar in the kitchen and used it to scoop up the icky creature.

Next came the horsefly. She got a second jar for that. Catching that was harder. It wasn't that she couldn't find one. The problem was that there were too many! They swarmed the beach.

Kelsey took a deep breath and ran right into a horde of them.

They landed on her skin. They buzzed in her ears. And they stung her.

When she finally clamped the lid on her jar, she had managed to trap three horseflies.

That left only one more fear.

A jellyfish.

Yuck.

Kelsey swam in the ocean searching for a jellyfish until her lips turned purple and her skin shriveled like a raisin.

But she still didn't have one when her parents called her in for dinner.

By the time she and Drew finished eating and headed back out, the sun was going down. And the beach was totally deserted.

"It's pretty weird being out here all alone," Kelsey commented. Then she thought about how weird it would be going out at midnight—when it was totally black outside. And a shiver ran down her spine.

"Yeah, it is creepy," Drew agreed. "Let's just hope

our parents don't catch us down here. If they do, Madame Valda's curse is going to be the last thing we have to worry about."

But Madame Valda's curse was the *only* thing that Kelsey was worried about. And if she didn't find a jellyfish, she was going to have to worry about it for the rest of her life.

Kelsey headed into the water.

Drew started to follow.

"You stay on the beach," she ordered. "Where you can see me."

"I think I should go with you," Drew argued.

"You can't," Kelsey reminded him. "I have to get the jellyfish myself."

Kelsey started walking out into the ocean. She scanned every inch of the water around her.

No jellyfish—anywhere.

She waded in farther and farther. The water grew deeper. And darker. And colder.

It's really scary out here, she thought as the water rose up to her shoulders.

She turned around to look for Drew. But she couldn't spot him.

She took a few more steps into the ocean—and suddenly the ocean floor dropped beneath her feet.

She plunged down. Down. Down.

Her arms shot up, out of the water. But her head remained beneath the surface.

75

The current pulled her down—deeper and deeper.

Kelsey struggled to break the water's surface. Struggled to breathe.

She kicked as hard as she could.

Her legs ached. Her lungs burned.

She needed air. She desperately needed air.

Coughing, gasping for breath, she finally burst free.

She gulped the cool night air, filling her lungs. Then she began to swim to shore.

But the water around her grew rough. She lost her rhythm and began to flail.

Concentrate! she told herself. *Concentrate!*

She kicked, hard. Her arms cut through the water. She swam and swam.

I must be close, she thought, panting. *I must be.*

But when she lifted her head, she froze.

She couldn't see the shore.

She couldn't see anything.

She was lost in a sea of darkness.

16

"**D**rew!" Kelsey screamed. "Drew!" But her cries were drowned by the crashing waves.

Kelsey's eyes darted around her. Trying to focus. Trying to spot a twinkle of light—any clue to show her the way to the shore.

But it was completely dark. So dark that she didn't see the wave forming behind her. The huge wave.

It crested and broke, catching her in a cyclone of foam.

It spun her upside down.

Then it whipped her out of the water.

And she spotted it—the shore. The giant wave had carried her closer to the beach.

"Drew!" Kelsey tried to scream. But a wave washed

over her, and she swallowed a mouthful of the salty sea.

Where was he? Her chest tightened.

Why couldn't she see him? Did he go for help?

Kelsey began to swim again. She was surprised to feel her strokes propel her easily through the water. And as the shore line grew closer, she began to feel better. The tightness in her chest eased.

And then the current changed.

Now it thrashed against her, propelling her sideways.

Directly in the path of a huge stone jetty!

"Nooooooo!" Kelsey screamed at the sight of the jagged rocks.

The waves roared in her ears. Her heart thundered in her chest.

She tried to swim against the force. She cast a glance at the jetty.

She was so close to it now.

So close to being pounded against its pointed, rough rocks.

And then she spotted Drew. Running along the jetty. Jumping from rock to rock.

The waves crashed around her, tossing her body. Tossing her inches from the craggy wall.

"Kelsey!" Drew shouted down. "I'll get help!"

"No!" she cried. "No time!"

A huge wave broke, thrusting her into one of the

rocks that jutted out. And a sharp pain shot through her leg.

I can't hold out any longer, Kelsey thought. She could feel the strength seep from her arms. Her legs.

Drew had to help her—now. In another moment she'd be smashed against the jetty.

She lifted her face to call to him one more time.

But he turned—and walked away.

17

The tide pelted Kelsey.

She threw her arms out—to soften the crash against the rough stones.

"Kelsey! Kelsey! Grab this!"

Drew!

He held out a pole—a pole with a red flag on the end. The kind lifeguards use to warn about rough seas.

Kelsey reached out. Stretching.

Grasping—grasping for the pole.

Drew held it out as far as he could.

Her fingertips grazed the end. She almost had it—but a wave broke over her, and the pole slipped from her hand.

She tried again—gripping it tightly this time. And Drew pulled her out of the churning sea.

As she sat on the jetty, gasping for breath, her fingers brushed against something. Something slimy.

She snatched her hand away.

A jellyfish.

She finally had her jellyfish.

"Drew," Kelsey whispered. "Drew, wake up. It's time to go."

Kelsey stood in the doorway of his room. She was wearing black jeans and a black hooded sweatshirt.

Drew sprang out of bed. "I'm up! I'm up!"

He was already dressed, in black jeans and a black sweatshirt too. He even had his sneakers on.

"Come on," Kelsey said as she tugged him out of bed. "It's almost a quarter to twelve. We have to move fast."

"Okay, okay," he muttered. "Do you have everything?"

"Uh-huh," Kelsey told him, patting her backpack. "Right here."

"Is everyone asleep?" he asked.

"Yep." Kelsey headed for the door. "So be quiet."

Kelsey tiptoed down the stairs to the front door. Drew followed.

She opened the door slowly so that it wouldn't

make a sound. Then she and Drew stepped out into the chilly night air.

"Make sure you leave it unlocked," Drew told her. "We need to get back in."

Kelsey nodded as she pulled the door closed behind them. "Let's go!" she cried, and the two started to run.

They didn't stop until they reached the boardwalk. "The gypsy camp must be this way." Kelsey turned to the left.

"Are you sure?" Drew asked.

"Well, it's probably near Gregor's fortunetelling place, right?"

"I guess," Drew said. "You should have asked him."

"No," Kelsey snapped. "*You* should have asked him. *I* wasn't allowed to ask any questions, remember?"

A flicker of light suddenly caught Kelsey's eye.

"Look." She pointed. "I was right!"

"Okay, okay," Drew admitted. "We'd better hurry."

Kelsey glanced at her watch. "Oh, no! It's three minutes to twelve! Let's—"

Drew grabbed Kelsey's arm and tugged her back into the shadows. A dark figure approached.

As it neared, Kelsey could see it was an old gypsy man—dressed in colorful, ragged clothing.

Kelsey stepped forward. She forced a smile. "We're looking for Gregor." Her voice squeaked.

82

"Then you must come quickly, child," he replied. He was missing almost all of his teeth, and his breath practically knocked Kelsey over. "Gregor is waiting for you. Come." The old man beckoned her with a spindly finger.

Kelsey wasn't so sure she wanted to follow him. But time was running out.

The old man led them under the boardwalk.

Kelsey had never been under the boardwalk. She felt as if she were in a huge cove. It was damp and dark—very dark. She could barely see the wooden planks high above her head.

She took a deep breath to steady her nerves. Her stomach lurched as the stench of dead fish filled her nostrils.

She wanted to turn back. But then she caught sight of a blazing fire up ahead.

As the three moved toward it, she could see gypsies—a crowd of gypsies—sitting in a circle around the crackling flames.

Their colorful clothing and golden jewelry glowed in the fire's light.

Inside the circle stood Gregor. His face flushed from the heat of the flames.

"So, you are here," he said as Kelsey and Drew approached. "Just in time."

All the gypsies rose and turned to stare at Kelsey

and Drew. Kelsey didn't like the feeling of all those eyes on her.

"Did you bring everything I commanded?" Gregor asked.

"Yes," Kelsey told him. "I've got them right here."

"Good," Gregor said. "Very good. Come then." He extended his hand. The gypsies parted, allowing Kelsey and Drew to step inside the circle.

Then Gregor clapped his hands together twice— and all the gypsies began to dance.

They danced around the fire, singing an eerie tune—in a language that Kelsey did not understand.

Kelsey didn't know what she was supposed to do. So she stood there and watched. Watched the gypsies whirl around her.

Kelsey recognized Zandra. She was dressed in her gypsy costume, wearing her long, dark wig. And as she danced with the others in the circle, she looked every bit as serious as the rest of them.

When Gregor clapped his hands again, the dancing and singing came to an abrupt stop. And everyone sat.

Gregor reached for an old leather-bound book lying close to the edge of the fire. "May I have all the items, please," he addressed Kelsey.

Kelsey reached into her backpack. First she pulled out the jar with the horseflies. She handed it to Gregor.

He took it without saying a word.

Then she gave him the jar that held the sand crab. He took that, too.

Kelsey had put the jellyfish in a plastic bag. But she still hated touching it. She tossed it over to Gregor quickly.

The last thing Kelsey pulled out of her backpack was the map.

Gregor spread all the items before him.

He turned the tattered pages of his book, searching for the proper chant.

Then he began, chanting in the same strange language Kelsey had heard before. And he rocked back and forth—in a deep, deep trance.

Kelsey wondered what Gregor was saying. But she didn't dare interrupt him.

"Is it over?" she whispered hopefully when Gregor finally stopped his strange song.

"Not yet," he answered. "For the curse to be broken, you must swallow your fears."

"What do you mean?" Kelsey asked.

Gregor nodded at the items on the ground in front of him. "You must swallow your fears," he repeated.

"Are you telling me that I have to eat those things?" Kelsey shrieked.

"Yes," Gregor told her. "It is the only way to break the curse."

18

"**N**o way!" Kelsey said.

Touching sand crabs and jellyfish was disgusting enough. Eating them was out of the question!

"We do not *have* to go on," Gregor declared.

"Yes, yes, we do," Kelsey moaned.

Gregor smiled. "Very well." Then he reached for the jar with the horsefly.

"You're going to do it?" Drew cried.

"I—I have to do it," Kelsey stammered. "I'm not letting that witch beat *me*."

"Are you ready to begin?" Gregor asked.

A hush fell over the bonfire.

Kelsey could hear the sounds of crashing waves in

the distance. The crackling of the flames before her. And the pounding of her heart.

"Yes," Kelsey forced herself to reply. "Only—couldn't we maybe start with the map first?"

Gregor nodded as he placed the jar down and picked up the map.

He tore a piece out of the map, right where Kelsey had circled her street. "Open your mouth."

Kelsey did, and Gregor placed the tiny piece of paper on her tongue. Then he began to chant.

Swallowing the map was really easy. It clung to the back of her throat for a only second. Then she managed to choke it down.

But as Gregor reached for the jar of horseflies, Kelsey's stomach heaved.

When he opened the jar, two of the horseflies escaped. Gregor plucked one of the wings from the horsefly lying in the bottom of the jar and held it out in front of Kelsey.

At least I don't have to swallow the whole thing. She sighed.

She stared at the wing, trying to convince herself that it wasn't going to be as terrible as she thought.

It's just a wing. A tiny, little wing. As harmless as a piece of cellophane.

Kelsey closed her eyes and opened her mouth. And

she told herself that that's exactly what it was—a little piece of cellophane.

The moment the wing hit her tongue, she pushed it back toward her throat. Then she swallowed quickly.

She didn't taste a thing. It almost felt like swallowing the skin of a peanut.

Only it wasn't the skin of a peanut. It was the wing of a horsefly. And Kelsey could feel it sticking in her throat. She swallowed and swallowed. But she couldn't make it go down.

She started to choke.

Just as she was about to ask for a glass of water, she saw Gregor reach for the sand crab.

She quickly gathered saliva in her mouth and forced the wing down in one big gulp.

Gregor lifted the crab and removed one of its legs. He dangled it in front of her.

Kelsey shut her lids tightly and tried not to think about it. Then she opened her mouth.

As soon as Gregor placed it on her tongue, she swallowed—hard and fast.

The crab leg scratched her throat as it went down.

Kelsey imagined that it was still alive.

Alive and wriggling back up into her mouth.

Kelsey slammed her hand over her mouth—so she wouldn't throw up.

"You have just one fear left," Gregor stated. Then he pulled out a jeweled knife and sliced off a chunk of the slimy, foul-smelling jellyfish.

The gypsies stared. Silently.

It seemed as if everyone stopped breathing.

Kelsey broke out into a sweat. She wiped her clammy palms on her jeans.

She tried to open her mouth. But she gagged.

"I can't," she cried as she turned her face away from Gregor.

"You must," Gregor told her. "Or the curse will always be with you."

"You can do it, Kelsey," Drew pleaded. "I know you can!"

She shook her head. "No," she told Drew. "I can't."

"Kelsey," Drew replied, "you have to."

Kelsey knew Drew was right. She had to try. "Okay," she said, inhaling deeply. "I'm ready."

Kelsey closed her eyes and held her nose. She opened her mouth. She told herself that if she swallowed it quickly, everything would be okay.

Gregor placed the quivering gunk in her mouth.

It oozed on her tongue.

She forced herself not to think about it. She closed her mouth around the bitter slime.

It tasted salty and fishy. Like eating rotten bait.

89

But the taste wasn't the worst part.

The worst part was how it felt in her mouth.

Slimy—like mucous.

Ooozing and sliding around on her tongue.

Swallow! Kelsey ordered herself. But she gagged again.

Swallow! This time the glob slipped down her throat. Slowly. Kelsey felt her stomach lurch.

She was sure she was going to vomit.

Swallow!

Kelsey had to swallow three times to force the quivering blob down her throat.

She opened her eyes slowly and smiled at Gregor. Drew beamed—as if she had just won an Olympic gold medal.

"You have done very well," Gregor congratulated her. "Very well, indeed. You are a brave girl. And you should be most proud of yourself."

"I am." Kelsey laughed. "I am!"

"You did it, Kelsey!" Drew exclaimed. "You really did it!"

"So, is that it?" Kelsey asked Gregor. "Is the curse all gone now?"

Gregor peered into his magic book. "No," he told Kelsey. "The curse has not yet been broken."

"What else do I have to do?" Kelsey wailed. "What else could there possibly be?"

"You must throw something belonging to Madame Valda into the fire," Gregor told her.

"You never told us that!" Drew yelled.

"Something belonging to Madame Valda!" Kelsey shrieked. "I don't have anything belonging to Madame Valda. I'm doomed," she told Drew. "I'm totally doomed."

19

"**There** must be another way!" Drew protested.

"No. No other way," Gregor stated.

"Maybe Madame Valda left something in your shack?" Drew turned to Zandra.

"Umm. Let me think. . . ."

"She didn't have anything except that stupid deck of cards," Kelsey interrupted.

"Kelsey!" Drew exclaimed. "That's it! The card! You still have the Fool card! *That* belonged to Madame Valda!"

Kelsey's face lit up. She started rummaging through her backpack to find it. "You're right! We *do* have something that belongs to Madame Valda." She laughed. "And here it is!" Kelsey pulled the Fool card out of her bag.

"I'm not sure this will work," Gregor said, taking the card from Kelsey to examine it.

"What do you mean?" Drew shouted. "Of course it will work. It's Madame Valda's card!"

"Yes, I know," Gregor started to explain. "But the book suggests using an article of clothing or jewelry."

"Yeah," Kelsey snapped. "But we don't have an article of clothing or jewelry. We have a card. Besides, the book doesn't say you *can't* use a card, right?"

"No," Gregor admitted, flipping through the pages. "It doesn't."

"Then this will work!" Drew exclaimed. "This will break the curse!"

Gregor handed the card back to Kelsey. "Yes," he agreed. "This should break the curse!"

The crowd of gypsies cheered.

Kelsey stared down at the card in her hand.

The Fool's haunting face grinned up at her. But this time Kelsey grinned back. She was going to break the curse. Now she was sure of it.

"Approach the fire," Gregor instructed as the crowd fell silent.

Kelsey took a deep breath. Then she stepped up to the flames.

The heat of the fire stung her cheeks—so she backed off, standing just close enough to toss in the card.

"Here goes," she whispered to herself.

She lifted her arm, ready to throw—and the fire began to crackle.

She lowered the card to her side. She glanced around. Then she began again.

But as she raised her arm, the fire's gentle flicker roared to a blaze.

Kelsey jumped back.

The flames soared higher and higher. Hot sparks shot out from their tops.

"What's going on?" she screamed at Gregor.

But Gregor didn't answer. Kelsey could see his face in the glow of the blaze. He looked terrified. He edged back—away from the circle of gypsies.

Kelsey moved in toward the flames.

I have to throw this card in! I have to!

"Hurry!" Drew shouted. "Throw it! Throw it before it's too late!"

Kelsey swung her arm back and—*BOOM!*

The fire exploded in her face. And the flames leaped out—leaped out to grab her!

She screamed and screamed.

And when she finally stopped, she heard a terrifying sound.

A sound she had heard once before.

A sound she would never forget.

The sound of Madame Valda's evil, haunting laugh.

20

Kelsey stared up. Up at the raging fire.

And gasped.

Madame Valda soared up from the center of the flames.

Her fiery body rose high above Kelsey. She loomed over them. Laughing madly.

"Again I face the Fool," she cackled.

Daggers of fire flew from her lips.

"What do we do?" Kelsey cried out to Gregor.

"I . . . I . . . don't know," he stammered, his eyes fixed on the evil gypsy woman.

"What do you mean, you don't know?" Kelsey screamed.

"He doesn't know because he is a fake!" Madame

Valda bellowed. "How can you believe in this gypsy clown—and not believe in Madame Valda!"

Kelsey whirled to face Gregor. He inched back again—farther and farther from the old woman.

"He is no gypsy!" Madame Valda roared. "He has no powers! There is nothing in his stupid, little magic book to help you."

Then Madame Valda pointed her finger at Kelsey. "Fool!" she cried.

A firebolt shot out from her fingertip—and the gypsies began to scatter.

"They are frauds," Madame Valda spat. "All of them. There is not one true gypsy among them."

As she spoke, she turned her hands upward. Pillars of black smoke burst from her palms.

"I'm out of here!" Zandra screamed and took off down the beach.

Madame Valda cackled at the sight.

"Come on, Kelsey." Drew grabbed Kelsey's arm. "Let's go!"

"I can't," Kelsey groaned. "If I don't face her now, I'll be under this curse forever."

Madame Valda laughed her evil laugh. "You are going to pay for angering Madame Valda yet again." Her eyes burned right through Kelsey. "Not only does this Fool insult me once, she enlists the help of more fools to insult me again!"

Kelsey spun around to face the other gypsies. But

no one remained. They had abandoned her—left her alone to fight the hideous witch.

"Did you really think you could get rid of my curse so easily?" Madame Valda crooned. "Well, think again! You will never get rid of it! Never!"

Madame Valda's laughter echoed through the night. Her hot red eyes bore into Kelsey.

"Kelsey!" Drew shouted. "Throw the card into the fire!"

"Go ahead, Fool," Madame Valda taunted. "Try to burn it! Try!"

"Stop calling me Fool!" Kelsey cried. Then she inched forward, her eyes glued to the ugly gypsy.

"Come, Kelsey." Madame Valda beckoned with a fiery finger. "Come closer to the flame!"

Kelsey stepped forward—and Madame Valda hurled a fireball at her feet.

Kelsey leaped away and fell.

"Come, Kelsey." Madame Valda laughed. "You can do it!"

"Kelsey!" Drew screamed. "Are you okay?"

Kelsey nodded, jumping to her feet.

"I have to try again!"

Kelsey glanced up at Madame Valda. The evil gypsy's eyes were closed!

"Throw it!" Drew screamed. "Throw it now!"

She must be tired, Kelsey thought.

"Now!" Drew screamed.

Kelsey swung her arm and hurled the card into the fire.

"Yes!" Drew's shouts echoed as Kelsey watched the card sail straight for the flames.

And then she felt it.

A strong wind against her face.

"Nooooo!" she shrieked as the card flew from the fire.

It rode the burst of hot air Madame Valda released from her chest.

Kelsey gaped in horror as her only hope blew away.

21

The Fool card soared past Kelsey.

Way above her head.

Way out of her reach.

Out—out toward the beach.

"Oh, no!" Kelsey cried. "It's headed for the ocean!" Kelsey and Drew tore down the beach after the fluttering card. It appeared as a dim white speck as it floated out—out to sea.

Madame Valda's laughter cut through the air, but Kelsey didn't turn back. She ran. Ran for her life.

"I can get it! I've got to!"

The beach was pitch black. Kelsey wanted to look down—to see where she was running. But she didn't.

She trained her eyes on the card. She could lose sight of it in a blink.

She ran faster. Faster.

But suddenly she felt heat at her back.

"She's chasing us!" Drew screamed.

Kelsey turned—and saw a huge ball of fire streak through the sky. It swooped down—and spun around her.

She stared in terror as Madame Valda soared up from the fireball's center. Dripping fire.

The flames licked at Kelsey's legs . . . arms . . . hair.

She threw her arms over her head and screamed.

"There is no way to escape me, Fool." Madame Valda's fiery breath hit the back of Kelsey's neck. "No way at all."

The card! Kelsey had lost sight of the card!

She jerked her head around. There it was! Dipping down—right in front of her.

Kelsey sprang up for it. And just as her finger brushed its tip, the gypsy's hot breath blew it away.

"Nooooo!" Kelsey screamed. "Nooooo!"

The card flipped and spun in the air.

Kelsey leaped for it.

The evil gypsy blew it again—blew it from her grasp.

"To the sea!" Madame Valda cackled. "To the beautiful *black* sea!"

The card swirled in front of Kelsey. It fluttered down in front of her face. Then rose up sharply.

Kelsey lunged for it. But it whirled around her.

Taunting her.

Then it sailed out to the shore.

Kelsey lunged again. Plunging in the cold, inky water.

"Say goodbye, you little fool!" Madame Valda shrieked. Then she threw her head back and roared with laughter.

And just as she did, Kelsey snatched the card from the air—and thrust it directly in the center of Madame Valda's flaming body!

"Here's your card back, Madame Valda!" Kelsey spat.

"Nooooooo!"

Madame Valda's screams rang out through the night. Her fiery form exploded in an enormous burst of light. And tore through the blackened sky.

Kelsey smiled as she watched the fire fade—as Madame Valda's features began to melt.

Her fiery figure shriveled up—smaller and smaller.

And then she disappeared in a puff of smoke.

22

"**N**o! No! Noooo!" Kelsey screamed when she heard the explosion.

"I won!" Drew shouted. "I won!"

Kelsey glared at the clown she had been aiming at. Its inflated balloon head bobbed from side to side.

She set down her water pistol, defeated. "Only because I let you win," she shot back.

Drew just laughed as the carnival barker handed him his prize—a giant pretzel. He broke it in two and gave her half.

"Thanks." She smiled. "What should we do next?"

"Let's go through the haunted house again," he suggested. "The Shadyside Carnival has the best haunted house!"

"That's because Shadyside is the best haunted town," Kelsey joked.

"I'm glad we made it back from the beach in time for the carnival," Drew said as the two headed for the haunted house ride.

"I'm glad we made it back at all," Kelsey replied.

"Oh, brother!" Drew pointed up ahead. "Look at that line!"

The line for the haunted house curved all the way around the ride twice.

"We'll be here forever," Kelsey complained. "Let's find something else to do."

"Like what?" Drew asked. Then he gasped.

"What?" Kelsey cried.

"Look!" He pointed to a sign that read "Gypsy Fortuneteller."

"That?" She laughed. "That's nothing. It's just a mechanical fortuneteller inside a glass box. Come on, I'll show you."

Drew hesitated.

"Come on!" she said again, tugging him over to the glass box.

As they neared it, a little girl slipped a quarter into the slot and waited for the mechanical fortuneteller to whirl around and tell her fortune.

She waited. And waited. And waited.

"This stupid thing is broken," the little girl complained, kicking the box. Then she gave up and walked away.

"See?" Kelsey said. "Nothing to be afraid of."

Drew stared at the box. "Just a machine," he said, breathing a sigh of relief.

Then she and Drew turned and walked away.

"Not afraid?" a voice called after them.

They stopped.

"Fool! Fool! Fool!" The voice cackled now. "Only a fool is not afraid!"